Rare *and* Wonderfully Made

KAMEO LLYN DOUGLAS

Improbable
PRESS

First published by Improbable Press in 2022

Improbable Press is an imprint of:

Clan Destine Press
www.clandestinepress.com.au
PO Box 121, Bittern Victoria 3918 Australia

Copyright © Kameo Llyn Douglas

All rights reserved. No part of this book may be reproduced or transmitted in any
form or by any means, including internet search engines and retailers, electronic or
mechanical, photocopying (except under the provisions of the Australian Copyright
Act 1968), recording or by any information storage and retrieval system, without
prior permission in writing from the publisher.

National Library of Australia Cataloguing-In-Publication data:

Kameo Llyn Douglas
Rare and Wonderfully Made

ISBN: 978-0-6489586-8-0 (pb)
ISBN: 978-0-6489586-9-7 (eb)

Cover artwork by © Kyndall Potts
Cover layout by © Willsin Rowe
Author photo by © Joshua Rodriguez/LMB Productions
Design & Typesetting by Dimitra Stathopoulos

Improbable Press
improbablepress.com

To Douglas and Nadine

For helping me become myself

1

Sherlock Now

"Bloody hell, Sherlock, what were you thinking?"

John is livid: furious and purplish-blue.

Aiming for a soothing tone, Sherlock says, "Sit down, John. I'll...make you a cup of tea. Your face looks—"

"Fuck my – shut it! You cannot, will not, ever again, speak to an officer like that! No matter how close to disaster, no matter how stupid they were. He was stupid, but Christ, that's not the point! You made him vomit!"

"It's not my fault he has a stomach condition, Jo—"

"He wasn't ill Sherlock, he was distraught! That child could've died, and he knew it! He didn't need to hear how badly he screwed up. The child's father certainly didn't need to hear it."

Sherlock stares, reviewing John's words, trying to understand. Why is John upset? Asking himself again *What did I do wrong?*

"Didn't you see what you were doing to her family? That poor rookie? Her father broke his jaw, Sherlock!"

With good reason. The officer had made a simple, nearly-fatal error. Sherlock had worked it out in time to save her. She was alive. He'd said nothing untrue. Yet, John was angry.

Again.

If it were anyone else, Sherlock wouldn't have noticed, let alone cared. But this is John. John should be happy. Instead, he looks like one of his arteries might burst.

Clueless as to how to make it better, Sherlock makes the tea, careful to get John's right. He puts it on the table, hoping John will sit. He waits, eyes flitting around. Play the violin? Leave? The longer he stands there, stricken, the more John deflates. He scrubs his hands over his face, and collapses onto the sofa.

"You don't get it, do you?"

Sherlock shakes his head, lost, and John forgives him. Or maybe forgiveness is the wrong concept. Maybe John needs to let go of unrealistic expectations.

"Come." He pats the sofa and Sherlock crosses the floor in three strides. He flops down, burrowing his face into John's shoulder, heartbreakingly grateful for the comfort of his husband. He curls his arms around him and John strokes his hair.

"I know you don't grasp it, love, but I don't either. How did you miss these lessons? Didn't anybody teach you not to hurt people's feelings? I don't remember much developmental psychiatry, but children start learning empathy before they leave the nursery. For god's sake, Mycroft may not feel it, but at least he knows when it's expedient to pretend! You think the way victims think, why don't you feel what they feel? I'm not blaming you; I'm trying to understand. Explain it to me."

And Sherlock thinks…

Where to begin?

2

Mycroft Then

Search term: Autism

In retrospect, Mrs Holmes realised she had been woefully unprepared for child-rearing, but, as ever to our species, the retrospection came much too late.

She was unfortunate, in a way, that Mycroft had been her eldest. He'd created false expectations for the cyclone that was her youngest. In both cases, the child was father to the man. Mycroft was cool, reserved, and studied, even as an infant, a pudgy, imperturbable thing that took one's measure in an instant. He schooled his reactions and used them to his advantage, keeping his cards close to the vest. He cried only when comfort was within reach, slept when conditions were conducive, and reserved his energy for maximum benefit, never exerting himself until his goal was attainable.

Mrs Holmes thoroughly approved of her self-contained baby and couldn't imagine why the other new mothers she encountered were so exhausted and frustrated with their offspring. Eventually she avoided them, whether it was out of a sense of guilt for her trouble-free post-partum experience, or the nagging sense that something might be wrong with her little angel, she would never be able to say. She and Mycroft withdrew into a placid co-existence, requiring nothing more than what the other was willing and able to give.

After Sherlock's arrival, Mummy would long for the days when she'd been bored.

Mycroft Now

Even for a place as devoted to silence as Mycroft's Diogenes Club, it was a quiet day.

He had placed himself strategically between the ambassadors of some Eastern European, formerly-independent, ethnically-segregated region, which preferred to be referred to as a nation, thank you very much, and the Republic which was nominally assisting in the region's return to a sovereign state, but was actually pillaging as rapidly as logistically possible. They pretended to ignore one another, one reading papers, the other deeply involved in his mobile.

Mycroft ignored the ambassadors completely, as he had already arranged for the dismissal of one and elevation of the other. He could not actually recall which was which but, in the end, it would turn out to be immaterial. The coup was already scheduled, the paperwork finalised earlier in the day.

He was more actively considering the decline in quality of the black currant scones. The fruit had been smaller and drier progressively over the course of the last week. He really was going to have to decide how much the power balance would shift from east to west if he made the radical change to cranberries. Although, he thought, how great was the danger of cranberry seeds getting stuck in his teeth? Calorie differences? He entered a reminder into his diary: Speak to the baker.

3

Sherlock Then

Search terms: DSM-V Diagnostic Criteria,
Autism Spectrum Disorder (ASD); DSM-IV Diagnostic Criteria, Asperger's Disorder;
Asperger's Syndrome; symptoms+ infancy;
extreme distress reactions; easily startled; regulation of arousal; soothability;
self-soothing

She should have guessed. Everyone warned her that first babies were late. However, Mycroft was born at 12:01 on his due date, with two hours of what the senior nurse called the "easiest labour I've ever seen." He was so quiet the doctor slapped his bottom to be sure everything was all right. Mycroft gave him such a howl of affronted disgust, he was rushed to intensive care "just to be on the safe side."

Sherlock, however, was born five days late, after twenty-seven hours of labour, and debuted with such ear-piercing shrieks of indignation, he was rushed to intensive care "just to be on the safe side." The senior nurse said she was amazed Mrs Holmes survived. Mummy claimed later on that she never quite recovered; he never gave her the chance.

Mycroft ate, slept, and met his developmental milestones according to some internal atomic clock. Sherlock wouldn't eat, never slept, and was delayed at every step. He wailed around the clock as if his skin was too tight for his body. He could not be soothed. For any respite at all, he had to be carried in full body contact at a smooth, rhythmic pace. He would occasionally drift off, but any attempt to put him down triggered a magnificent tantrum.

He spent most nights in his parents' bed.

```
Search terms: Asperger's syndrome+ devel-
opmental delays; motor skills; oral-mo-
tor+ control; feeding problems; failure to
thrive; dysregulated breastfeeding
```

The nannies came and went so quickly that Daddy gave up trying to remember their names. Mycroft kept a notebook with lists and sketches, but Daddy was there so rarely, sometimes he never even met them.

Mrs Holmes described them according to their staying power. "This looks to be a three-day nanny," or "the one who stayed a month."

Mycroft would pipe in, "That was Flora, Mummy. Sherlock liked her." And Mycroft, at seven, manoeuvred behind the scenes to usher the most inadequate of them out more quickly. Although Sherlock was quite capable of it himself.

As Sherlock failed to thrive, Mummy dwindled away beside him. At his six-month visit, Sherlock had failed to gain sufficient weight, and the paediatrician switched him to formula and a cup, since he refused to drink from a bottle. Nannies stayed a bit longer after that, but Sherlock was passed around the household staff and Mycroft, who took him out in his pram every afternoon, prattled at him constantly.

Mrs Holmes stopped looking in the baby books. Sherlock was always behind schedule, and the suggestions never worked. Mycroft, however, never doubted. When Mummy bemoaned Sherlock's failure to sit, he would prop the baby up and give him pep talks, at which he giggled and waved his fists. Mycroft had endless faith in his baby brother.

Search terms: Asperger's syndrome or autism
spectrum disorder+ food selectivity; sensory
sensitivity; eating problems

The paediatrician insisted on weekly weigh-ins for scrawny little Sherlock and ordered Mrs Holmes to transition him to solid foods as quickly as possible. "We need to get more calories into him."

Baby food was an immediate failure, even the most palatable, like sweet potatoes and applesauce. He screwed up his perfect, pink, little mouth and shook his wee head and would not be enticed. Sometimes Mycroft would make him laugh so he could slip a spoonful in, but when Sherlock deduced the foul trickery, he turned his face from his beloved older brother.

Mycroft cried.

Due to the complete lack of baby fat (Mummy thought nostalgically of Mykie's chubby thighs and belly rolls), Sherlock suffered more gravely from the average childhood afflictions: ear infections, stomach viruses, fever, anything that put him off his usual meagre feed sent him to hospital for life-threatening dehydration. Getting medicine into him required staff restraining every limb.

Unbeknownst to anyone, Sherlock's teeth had come in. None of the usual signs had appeared: no drooling or teething, and if there was any extra discomfort, it wouldn't have registered amidst the general unpleasantness of Sherlock's constant fretting.

Then began a lifelong quest for foods he would eat. There were never very many. He refused to try most. He survived for five years on milk, eggs, and bread.

Sherlock Then

About five years after he became a consulting detective, Sherlock had given chase. It was pointless really, there was nowhere for the suspect to go. Bleeding, he would most likely have collapsed within a few blocks. But Sherlock was like a greyhound sighting a rabbit; when the man turned to run, Sherlock tore after him, Lestrade screaming his name. Unfortunately, he was faster than the amped up suspect and when he caught him, he also caught the swipe of a switchblade across his abdomen. The adrenalin high was such that he refused to believe that anything serious had happened and had to be wrestled onto the gurney and yelled at by Mycroft via mobile to get him to hospital.

Mycroft met them there and added his voice to the cacophony all directed towards the squirming squid of a man, fussing like a child.

"I don't need stitches! Just tape it and let me out of here! This is kidnapping! You're keeping me against–"

A commanding voice, not overly loud, low, but authoritative, called out, "That's enough." It cut through the bickering and scuffle and miraculously froze Sherlock mid-struggle. Everyone turned toward it. It came from a middle-sized man of strong build, but thinner than he ought to be, thick through the jaw and neck. He was unremarkable except in bearing.

John Watson's transition from Afghanistan to London was less than smooth. Normal life provided long periods of quiet, but lacked the punctuation of head-spinning, gut-wrenching moments of terror. He'd thought he would be grateful, but somehow the numbness of the day-to-day left John empty. There were times he couldn't remember why he and his comrades had looked forward to coming home.

Therapy helped. It was someone to talk to, someone who didn't judge his nostalgia for the sanctioned violence. She was a bit pushy about his finding a new role for himself, but he tolerated it. At least it was an obligation. She was a woman who cared, and John Watson was not a man to miss an appointment.

John was offered a new purpose by an old friend from medical school, who found him a position in the A&E at St Bart's. He was good at it. Steady. Unshakeable in fact. He exuded a calm competence that soothed frantic parents and screaming children alike. Nurses jockeyed to be on his shift because things just went more smoothly. Everyone was more careful, paid more attention, but the work felt

RARE AND WONDERFULLY MADE

easier. And his quiet compliments, "You handled that perfectly," or "You're quite good at that, you know," or even a simple "Well done," were more sought after than an extra cigarette break.

When he heard the ruckus, John handed off the plastering of a fractured forearm to his assistant. The man shrugging off his nurses' attempts to cleanse the still bleeding wound was so manic that John wondered if he was under the influence of some substance. When he caught a glimpse of the injury, there was no doubt that it needed stitching and he cut through the noise with his officer's voice. He stood ramrod straight, hands behind his back, and continued. "Thank you, Philip, I'll take it from here."

"Good luck," said the nurse and stepped away from the table with a final glare at Sherlock, who hadn't taken his eyes off Dr J. Watson, as his nametag read.

"Now. I have a six-year-old next door who's bearing up under a broken arm with more pluck than you are. The sooner you behave yourself, the sooner we'll get the stitches done."

Sherlock opened his mouth and found himself cut off immediately.

"Taping won't do, so hush up, lie down, and let me do my job."

The room was silent, Sherlock in careful consideration of the man who had chastised him, and everyone else in astonishment, as he actually lay down. Mycroft was particularly shocked. Sherlock hadn't allowed himself to be silenced in years, let alone done as a stranger had bidden.

Mycroft watched without moving his head, afraid to shatter the crystallised tension, nearly visible, between them.

The doctor nodded, snapping his gloves off and washing at the sink.

"Gentlemen, I detest paperwork, so we'll agree that the patient experienced a…construction accident, not a knife fight?" He glanced between the three men, unsure who would decide. Lestrade nodded at Mycroft, who glared at Sherlock, who shrugged dismissively.

Mycroft nodded at the doctor who traced the flow of power, enjoying the subtlety, developed through long practice, he surmised.

Sherlock had been working with his brother's husband for nearly a decade, but was still able to both dazzle Lestrade with brilliance and work him into a lather with ease. Even together Mycroft and Lestrade could barely contain Sherlock, but given the ever-present memory of him pale and lifeless in a hospital bed, they much preferred this struggle.

"Where did you serve, Iraq or Afghanistan?"

Doctor Watson startled suddenly as he was pulling on new gloves. "Sorry, what?"

"You've only recently returned from the middle east, you're practically a poster-boy for the military, army or marines, army I'm thinking, marines probably too hardcore for a healer, your tan is demarcated by your sleeve line, you read the room like an officer, and you could stand to put on twenty pounds. You also miss the battlefield."

John stared.

"How…how did you know that?" He looked at Lestrade who smiled knowingly, and Mycroft, who was still scowling at Sherlock.

"Hmm. That's disappointing. For a few moments I thought you might be wittier than you look. I told you how I knew, were you not listening?"

Lestrade looked at Mycroft. "Could you step outside for a minute, love? I'd like to hit him and I don't want you to have to lie about it. We're safe in court, spousal privilege, but I think they could compel you at the inquest."

Mycroft answered, "Nonsense, I'll hold him down."

They were interrupted by a deep, rolling laugh, which increased in volume. All three turned to look at John, who laughed until tears filled his eyes.

"Thank you, all three of you. I haven't laughed so hard since I got home."

Mycroft's head tilted slightly and Lestrade looked at him out of the corner of his eye. Sherlock frowned.

"You're not insulted? You're still going to treat me?"

"It was Afghanistan and I treated people there who tried to kill me. *While* they were trying to kill me. You develop a fairly thick skin. And you're so puny, I could lay you flat if I had to."

Sherlock swallowed. Most doctors would've stormed out by now. Many had.

The ex-Major hadn't budged.

"We've had our fun, and there are other patients, so, will you lie still, or do I have to strap you down?"

Sherlock swallowed again and shook his head.

"There's a good lad. Now, the wound is deeper than I'd usually suture with a local, but it would be less complicated." His mouth slightly open now, Sherlock sat silent.

"He's starting to look pale. Either of you his proxy?" John looked at Lestrade, who pointed at Mycroft.

"Can he handle a local? He seems stoic."

"Excessively so. A local would be preferable." Mycroft took the doctor aside and opened his suit coat to extract his wallet. He showed John the contents.

"Ah. Well. No pressure."

Mycroft smiled with his mouth. "To the contrary, Doctor, I'm quite impressed. Not many people can…subdue my brother." Mycroft cast his eyes sideways at said brother, who was positively glowering at him now.

"In fact, I think you might be just the kind of positive influence he needs. And I suspect the room in his flat would more than suit your current needs. Consider it a gift from her majesty in appreciation of your service and sacrifice."

"What – how–"

Mycroft carefully and pointedly returned his wallet to his pocket.

Sherlock closed his eyes and shivered.

It had nothing to do with how much he'd bled.

Once John moved in with Sherlock, they settled into the routine of no routine. John was a calming influence when Sherlock would have started getting into trouble, and mitigated his reckless behaviour while working. He was a steadying hand and tireless cheerleader. Mycroft was proud of this particular machination, partly because Sherlock put up only pro forma resistance. He complained feebly to Mrs Hudson, but told her it was her decision. She said that John had already come by with Mycroft, she found him delightful, and was sure he would be a positive influence. Sherlock considered his protestations sufficient to have established credibility.

Years earlier, she'd found teenage Sherlock unconscious on her doorstep. She checked his wallet to find Mycroft's number, and also learned it was his eighteenth birthday. She dumped a bucket of water on him and when he jumped up spluttering, she said, "Happy birthday. Go shower. You stink."

She rescued him twice more but the third time scolded Mycroft for losing him.

"I could understand once, maybe twice, but honestly I'd keep better track of him than you and your hounds. He obviously needs supervision. He seems to be finding his way here regularly. At least he won't be on the street. There's a large flat to let upstairs but I can't imagine he has that many belongings."

4

Sherlock Then

Search terms: Asperger's or autism+ response
to pain, sensory processing+ pressure, touch
sensitivity; proprioception; pain percep-
tion; hyporesponsiveness to sensory stimuli

Struggling to provide, let alone figure out what Sherlock needed, Mummy floundered, grasping at straws and feeling inadequate. Everyone reassured her that he would grow out of it (whatever it was), but as Sherlock grew, his infantile crankiness bled into childhood.

It couldn't be colic anymore, although no one had ever been able to explain what colic was except lots of crying. Paradoxically, he seemed impervious to unpleasant bodily sensations like cold, hunger, and pain. They didn't seem to affect him. He refused to wear layers of clothing, no matter the temperature. He went barefoot into November. He could be falling asleep on his feet, but resisted going to bed. He never felt hungry and needed reminders to eat. The paediatrician hypothesised that he'd had infantile reflux and associated eating with discomfort. Perhaps he'd deactivated his hunger neurons permanently.

Sherlock broke his arm. Twice. The first time required surgery. The second, he apparently felt no pain. He passed two days holding his arm unnaturally still. Nobody noticed but Mycroft.

"Go 'way, Mykie! Stop poking!"

"Hold still, you!" Mycroft scolded. Sherlock obeyed (no one else.) Mycroft poked and Sherlock yelped. X-rays revealed a hairline fracture.

Mummy was dismayed. "Why didn't you say something, Sherlock?"

"It didn't hurt till Mykie broke it!"

He frequently didn't notice injuries until someone pointed out the bleeding.

```
Search terms: Asperger's or autism+ sensi-
tivity; reactivity to tactile+ perception,
stimulation; hyperresponsive; hyperreac-
tivity to sensory input; sensory modulation
disorder; tactile defensiveness
```

Sherlock clearly felt some things.

Anyone who spent any time with him saw his hyperreactivity. Some sensations were overwhelming, out of proportion to the experiences of others. The undetectable stimuli of everyday life tortured him. He perceived some ordinary environmental conditions as extreme. Excessive light, some sounds, certain distinctive odours, some sensory aspects that were completely benign to people around him triggered extreme responses, even tantrums.

He covered his ears to block out sounds that no one else could hear without searching for them.

Lullabies made him cry. The buzz of a fluorescent light in the room next door could drive him to distraction.

The aroma of hazelnut coffee drifting out of a shop's open door could make him vomit. His food peculiarities were legendary. The family took to sending out a scout to clear a restaurant for Sherlock before committing to a meal.

They taught him to carry headphones and sunglasses to block out stimuli that they couldn't avoid.

He allowed very few people to touch him and avoided crowds entirely.

He couldn't stand dirty hands and wouldn't touch anything like clay, or mud, or bread dough.

He was stoic in the face of jabs, but blood pressure cuffs set him hyperventilating. He couldn't tolerate tags in his shirts. He wouldn't wear long sleeves or socks.

"My feet can't breathe!"

Sherlock knew that he was difficult. He saw the accommodations his parents made for his comfort. He believed they 'loved' him. He knew that Mummy and Daddy loved each other but wasn't sure how he knew, and he tried to analyse their behaviours. There were the affectionate words and pet names for one another, their private shorthand that they would never explain.

"That's our secret, Sherlock. Grown-ups are allowed to have secrets from their children."

He saw it in the way Mummy missed him. She was never at her best when Daddy was gone, and he was gone very often. Mycroft and the staff stepped up to manage the household and Sherlock did his best to stay on an even keel. He spent as much time as he could outside, the space and quiet soothing his soul and allowing Mummy to regroup.

Sherlock tried to follow his parents' dynamics as they prepared to separate. They were predictable in how they planned to try to spare each other anxiety.

She would tell the boys, "We must be brave, so he doesn't worry about us." When Daddy called, Mummy perked up and spoke cheerfully, no matter what had been going on lately. She never discussed any of the troubles that might be happening while he was gone. Sherlock could not understand her bravado.

She never let him know that she would miss Daddy, but Sherlock knew she would, and Daddy certainly knew. He was always worried about her well-being while he was gone and asked Mycroft and Sherlock to look after her in his absence. He called and spoke to each of them every night and Sherlock worked hard to behave appropriately so that he could report his success.

"I was steady as she goes today, Daddy. And restrained! Even though it was pasta day, we had rice, but I was flexible and I didn't tantrum or even make a fuss. I said, 'Hmm, that's unexpected,' and ran around the house and then I came back and ate the rice and Mummy said she was very proud of me. That was self-control, wasn't it, Daddy? I was responsible?"

"Very responsible, little man. Mummy was right to be proud of you, and I'm proud of you as well. Keep up the good work. Pass me to Myke, now, will you?" He would always double-check with Mycroft before he finally signed off. It was Myke's responsibility to let him know if Mummy were starting to falter.

"Keep an eye on her. Make sure she eats and drinks enough water. Have Sherlock get her out to the garden when the weather permits. You boys are my backup."

Sherlock saw the sacrifices and compromises his parents made for one another, and how they altered their behaviour to save the other discomfort or anxiety. How did they know what the other needed? It couldn't be pure observation, there was no one in the world who could observe more carefully than Sherlock. Even Mycroft conceded that. He watched and studied them and even admired them, but doubted very much that he would ever be able to recognise what another person might need from him. He could hardly understand his own needs.

What was it that drove them to care for one another so deeply? There was no genetic connection between them. They shared offspring, was that enough? When Sherlock had matured, he understood that there might be biological imperatives that would compel his parents to care for him despite his peculiarities, but between them the only connection he could see was their affection for one another. They enjoyed being in each other's company. They took pleasure in the other's happiness, even at the cost of their own. Why?

He knew that the things he enjoyed were unlike most of those that other people enjoyed. The things they enjoyed were mysterious to him. It was difficult at best for him to be around other people. He saw himself as a lifelong bachelor.

When Daddy returned, the household breathed deeply in relief. Daddy found Sherlock a delight to be with, his every act intriguing. Even his tantrums were an interesting puzzle to be worked out. His matter-of-fact acceptance and strategising complemented Mummy's nurturing support. Although he couldn't describe it, there was something very appealing about his parents when they were together, and he knew that their harmony worked to his benefit. It seemed like everything they did supported each other's efforts.

He couldn't imagine finding another person who would motivate him to compromise his own wants and needs. He would never be able to expend the energy necessary to interpret or deduce what might make someone happy. In a practical sense he could appreciate the convenience of having someone to look after you no matter how irritating you were sometimes. He knew he was irritating, but they never made him feel like he was. They were more than the sum of their parts when it came to managing him. They handed him off to one another in a complex sleight of hand, with moves that would impress a footballer. It was comforting to see how they fit each other, anticipating one another's moves and their synchrony. Maybe that was love? Although he would never use the word himself, it was a thing of beauty.

5

Sherlock Now

Before he and John became what they were, Sherlock frowned at love. At best, it distracted from clear thinking. Romance was a good place to begin an investigation, but that just proved his point: love was treacherous. It complicated lives. Passion turned supposedly ethical people into criminals.

John discovered the truth gradually; Sherlock found love frightening. At first John thought his disdain was honest, that he truly believed that love would be nothing more than grit in his sensitive logical instrument. The longer they were flatmates the more John understood that Sherlock found emotional vulnerability threatening. Love was inexplicable; therefore, it was dangerous.

Their compatibility was apparent immediately. The physical attraction was almost as immediate, but their fear of disturbing what had become the most important relationship in their lives kept them from acting on it. The more they worked together, the more at ease they were, and their trust in one another was implicit. Their affection for one another was palpable, but Sherlock was so consistent in his disregard for romantic love, that John felt he had no choice but to suppress what Sherlock would have considered his animal instincts. Sherlock's heedlessness for his bodily needs was well-known.

But the intimacy of their relationship wouldn't be denied, and the more Sherlock opened his heart, the more John desired his body.

Yet, because this was nothing like a courtship, John resigned himself to the fact that Sherlock was saving himself for…something.

John knew there was a mutual attraction. There was no mistaking the crackle of sexual tension between them. Their intimacy deepened, but Sherlock could not relax enough to be touched. The wide range of Major John Watson's sexual conquests had never included anyone as skittish as Sherlock. John's initial attempts to express physical affection spooked Sherlock like a feral cat.

Even with Mrs Hudson, he'd stiffen almost imperceptibly at her hand on his shoulder. He'd kill for the woman, but her touch triggered a reflex he couldn't suppress. John's gut instincts were to avoid direct conversation about it. Sherlock already knew it was a problem, so John developed a plan of gradual desensitisation, a kind of therapy or allergy treatment. He would introduce the trigger stimulus at such diminished strength that it wouldn't initiate a reaction, then gradually increase the intensity. Desensitisation was fairly effective for phobias of all kinds. Though John was very subtle, he wanted Sherlock to notice. He began to decrease the distance between them, an inch at a time, backing off before Sherlock's anxiety flared up. He brushed up against him and withdrew before Sherlock registered the contact. He was determined to continue until proximity was bearable.

Sherlock himself couldn't identify his anxiety.

Was it closeness he was afraid of? He had no data. No one had really touched him since childhood. It took ages for him to realise he felt something for John   he simply had no idea what it was. Once he was aware of it, things became complicated. What was the difference between attraction and sentiment? Which came first? Did it matter? Did he have to understand the feelings? Should he allow them to continue? Could he control them? He had always been successful in ignoring sensations in the past. What were the consequences of acting on them? He hadn't had a friend since… had he ever had one? He couldn't afford to lose the one he had. The physical sensations were not entirely unpleasant, but he wasn't sure that pursuing them was worth risking what they had. Whatever that was. Because whatever it was, it was better than being alone. It was good actually, something he'd never thought possible.

Of course, he noticed what John was doing. It was sort of endearing and he'd die before he'd admit it, but it might be working.

John tried to explain the similarity between sexual excitement and anxiety. Sherlock frequently suffered from sensory overload. When it was interwoven with new emotions, there was no wonder he was befuddled.

So John helped Sherlock process the link between the physical drives and their emotional roots. The bodily sensations were new because the sentiment was new. That desire to use John's shampoo? Inspired by the connection to the idea of John. The tingling when they brushed against each other? The sexual attraction sprang from their emotional connection.

"John, if this is love, I can't do it. Forty-five percent of it feels awful! My pulse is racing, I'm sweating – aren't those symptoms of acute myocardial infarction?"

John took many deep breaths and talked him through it. "That's a stress response, Sherlock. It's the same way you feel when you're about to solve a case. It's what you tell yourself that frames the experience. When we're chasing after someone who might shoot at us, how does it feel?"

Sherlock thought briefly and wistfully of heroin, then of John. He smiled at him warmly. He regretted (almost) nothing.

John grinned back. "Honestly, could you tell the difference between being terrified and being thrilled? They both come from adrenalin flooding your system. We, you and I, confuse anxiety and excitement constantly. It's what we live for! It nauseates most people. Of course, it's going to frighten you. But you'll rise to the challenge. It will be invigorating! Think of it as facing a threat – a bullet!"

"Loving someone is not nearly as dangerous as chasing a criminal over a rooftop. You're going to have to trust me. We just have to figure out how to keep the sensations from overwhelming you. Maybe you need to separate the input from the emotions. You've experienced the sensations before."

Sherlock looked at him suspiciously. "Which sensations?"

John was confused. "Aren't we talking about...touch, Sherlock? Skin on skin. Fingers in your hair? When you – or someone expresses their love in a physical way?"

Blank stare.

"Sex. We're talking about sex. You've had orgasms. That's what we're talking about."

Sherlock scoffed. "Of course, I've had orgasms. Just...never with...another person."

John nodded, trying not to let the shock show on his face. "Right. So of course, it's a little intimidating. You shouldn't feel any embarrassment over that. Perfectly normal when you're facing a new...challenge. We'll just figure out how to make it less threatening. Not that it won't still be challenging," he said quickly when he saw Sherlock's eyes widen.

"Perhaps if all the sensations don't come at once. Maybe we can piece them out over time; put you in charge of them? Or we could turn it all over to you – allow you to control the amount of stimulation. No matter how we proceed, you're still going to have to be brave."

Sherlock Then

It was a tradition in the Holmes family for the children to go to summer camp so that they could learn to do summer-camp-like things, such as swim, canoe, sail, and start fires (Sherlock was already an expert). It was clear to everyone early on that this would not be an option for Sherlock.

"Nevertheless," said Daddy, "no Holmes child will go out into the world lacking essential life-saving skills."

Between the three of them, Daddy, Mummy, and Mycroft

managed to instruct Sherlock, who was the ideal student, in most of what Daddy considered to be mandatory. Sherlock desperately wanted to learn to sail the little Sunfish dinghy that his grandparents kept at the lake house. The geometry of it fascinated him and he longed to be able to sail out onto the quiet and stillness of the lake. However, no sailing would be possible until he learned to swim. There was a family discussion after an assigned reading on the leading causes of accidental death among children and Sherlock was convinced of the necessity. No one felt qualified to teach him and Daddy held fast. "This is a job for a professional, Sherlock. It is a technical skill. We are not taking any shortcuts. You will learn the correct techniques from an instructor and establish good habits from the beginning."

The first class was disastrous. He never made it into the water.

Mummy was more distressed than usual. "He wouldn't even tell me what was wrong! He said, 'All of it,' then shut down. What could I do? We came home."

All parties withdrew to regroup. But Mycroft, as usual, surveyed the conflict from a distance and took initiative.

Late that night, he asked Sherlock for permission to climb into bed with him. "Tell me what happened. What was the problem that kept you from doing this thing that you want very much?"

"Too many things."

"Can't you remember? Just start with the first."

"That's not what I meant." Mycroft heard the unspoken "Stupid."

"I remember them. It was that they were all together at the same time! The lockers banged, the room echoed, I had to take off my clothes, the floor was cold and slippery, I had to take a shower, there were too many people, it smelled, it was too dark, then it was too bright, the children—"

"Ahhh. Too many things."

His hand slid over the sheet and crept into Mycroft's. "All at once."

Mycroft said, "Problem solved. Simple. We'll handle them one at a time, that's all."

"We will?"

"Trust me, little brother. We will get you into that boat."

Mycroft and Daddy went to the next class without him. They did reconnaissance on the locker room and the pool. They spoke to the aquatics director to explain the situation and interviewed instructors. Financial arrangements were made, and 'swimming' lessons began.

Three days a week Sherlock went to the pool. The first day he and Mycroft met the instructor in the lobby and together they wrote up a checklist of steps necessary to pass the swimming test. The first item was 'Go into the locker room.' The last was 'Pass the swimming test.' In between were things like, 'Experiment with footwear,' and 'How to adjust water temperature in the shower,' and 'Learn to swim.' Sherlock was granted sole authority of the document. He made all decisions on advancing or retreating, adding or subtracting items, and when a lesson was over for the day. Raymond, the instructor, was chosen for his easy-going nature and infinite patience. He was comfortable with Sherlock's long silences and 'little professor' personality. He began every lesson by offering Sherlock several options, then waiting for Sherlock to tell him which he'd like.

They moved very slowly.

It was four weeks before they entered the water. A great deal of that time was spent in conversation, with Sherlock lecturing and asking questions about things like fluid dynamics and buoyancy.

Raymond approached each impediment with gravity. He adopted Sherlock's logical methods and kept track of their progress, which was so motivating, Sherlock looked forward to lessons. During one session they looked for a pair of non-slip shoes that could be worn into the pool. They solved the noise problem with earplugs he could keep in a zippered pocket of a warm thermal wetsuit that hugged his skin, eliminating the loose, wet fabric of trunks clinging and flapping against his legs. They discovered an extra-large bathing cap, that accommodated his hair without tugging and covered his ears, during the search for shoes. They observed so many lessons from the side of the pool that the actual learning to swim was an afterthought. Sherlock picked up the mechanics in two weeks and then simply had to build stamina. "He really taught himself. It's like he memorised the lessons. He knew exactly what he needed to learn, and just told me what to teach him. Easiest student ever! Once we nailed down the trivia. One step at a time, that's all."

The swim test itself was anticlimactic. Sherlock climbed out of the water and shook Raymond's hand. "Are you available next week? I had a dream about floating in the lake and looking at the sky and I would like to learn the backstroke."

6

Sherlock Now

"What do you mean I control the stimulation?" Sherlock asked warily.

"Maybe it's too much input. Maybe you need to regulate the flow of incoming data."

"You'd let me lead the whole thing?" Sherlock didn't try to hide his scepticism, but the hint of interest in his voice was enough for John to pursue the thought.

"Why not? You decide what we'll do and when, like always. Like... maybe you just watch me first. Or maybe you just touch me. Or maybe I touch you with one finger. Or maybe pick something you want to start with and you, we, make a plan. Change it as we go. It's not like there's a deadline or schedule. Or there could be if you wanted."

"What if you get frustrated...or tired of waiting?"

"It's been two years, Sherlock. I'm not in any rush, are you? If frustration were an issue, I'd be gone by now. I haven't had a date in, what, four years? You know I have a wank in the shower when I need to. It wouldn't be any different from how it is now. We'd just be trying something new. Look, no matter what happens, I'm not going anywhere. I've made my choice. It's you. I love you. As you are and as you will be. This is where I belong.

"If we never go further, if sex turns out not to be what you want, I've already learned to adapt to it. So, there's no pressure. If you'll have me, we'll take the rest of our lives to figure out how we're going to be together and however that is, that's how I want it.

So, you're in charge. You tell me if or when you're ready. In the meantime, if it's okay with you, I'd like to keep trying to get closer. Just close enough to touch." He took Sherlock's hand and touched their fingertips together. Sherlock rolled his eyes and John knew he was reassured.

"We can approach it like one of your experiments. We could measure your reaction to any attempts to decrease distance. See if it's something you're willing to try. Remember, we can always just leave things as they are."

John printed up some articles on systematic desensitisation. He continued to inch his way closer, and they developed a system whereby Sherlock could quantify his anxiety to John's advances. John also began to be a little less considerate. He had always been respectful of Sherlock's sensibilities, staying clothed around him, despite Sherlock's lack of modesty. Now he pushed the limits, going shirtless, brushing against him in the kitchen, not closing the door while taking a bath.

John also became much more forward in identifying when he, himself, felt turned on and what he thought the reasons were. One night after he'd had just enough to drink, he proposed an experiment. He wanted to know how much intimacy Sherlock could tolerate, and assuming that went well, see how turned on he could make Sherlock without actually touching him. Sherlock agreed in the name of science. And as they had with anxiety levels, they quantified the rating system.

List of Things to Try to See How Much John and Sherlock Can Turn Each Other on Without Actually Touching (Without Any Surprises)

- John stripping for Sherlock and vice versa
- John stripping Sherlock and vice versa
- John wanking in front of Sherlock and vice versa
- Sherlock watching John in the shower and vice versa

- John videotaping himself for Sherlock to watch and vice versa
- Watching porn together and vice – never mind
- Exchanging photos if the videos are too much
- Reading erotica to one another
- Writing erotica for one another
- John recounting some of his adventurous sexual exploits
- Sending explicit texts
- Phone sex
- Writing a list of fantasies for one another
- Sleeping in the same bed
- Getting drunk to lower inhibitions
- Bathing one another (with sponges)
- Walking around naked

John told him, "It may just come down to a matter of biology."

John was right.

In the end, biology won out. Sherlock was walking around in a perpetual state of agonising arousal. And John absolutely refused to touch him. He actually began to increase the distance between them, and Sherlock found it maddening. He was quite blatant about it. "It's a well-known and very old strategy, Sherlock. Back to the Garden of Eden. We always want what we cannot have. I am playing hard to get."

He walked around the flat with his pyjama trousers hanging low on his hips, wrapped in a towel or in pants only. He stroked himself leisurely during telly time. He was louder than absolutely necessary while engaging in his morning wanks. He sought Sherlock out during his, trying to catch him in the act. He dug his dog tags out of his trunk and made sure to fuss with them as much as possible. He bought a couple of shirts a few sizes too small. Sherlock was a twitching mess, jumping out of his skin. It reminded him of heroin and why he had given it up.

Then the devilish doctor imposed a rule. "How badly do you want this? Badly enough to give up touching yourself? "

"Badly."

Sherlock cleared his throat and wiped his hands on the back of his trousers. "Very, very badly."

With the no-touching rule still in effect, John presented himself to Sherlock as an experimental subject. He encouraged him to touch him however he liked. To keep him distracted from any dangerous emotions, John ordered him to objectively record John's responses to the different types of stimulation. He hoped an external focus could lull him into security, perhaps enough to liberate him from the tyranny of his own fear.

Allowing him complete control over John and allowing him to observe John's ability to integrate his physical and emotional reactions, would serve as a model and might give him the courage he needed to be the recipient of such intense focus. John would narrate his experience at every step. He took off his clothes and lay down on the bed. Sherlock asked, "What should I do?"

John responded, "Whatever you like. Start at the top. "

"Excellent plan. Work my way down."

John swallowed and resolved to remain as still as possible. He reconsidered. "Are you sure you don't want to restrain me, Sherlock? I'm afraid I might lose control."

"Why would you lose control?"

"I'm attracted to you. I'm naked. You're going to touch me. I'm going to be aroused. I'm going to want to touch you."

Sherlock licked his lips and looked down at him, spread out like a banquet.

Sherlock took John's heart and respiratory rate and began noting it down.

John interrupted him. "Look."

Sherlock did and John's eyes flicked down to his cock which had begun to take a decided interest in the proceedings. Sherlock's eyes widened. "How? Why?"

"It's you. You arouse me. It might be hard—" Sherlock snorted and John ignored him. " –to keep from reaching out. I don't want to startle you. I know how…" He didn't want to use the word frightening. Sherlock was the bravest man he knew. "… unprecedented this is for you. It's going to be intense. Maybe you should tie me up."

"You would let me restrain you." It wasn't a question exactly.

John looked irritated. "What wouldn't I let you do, moron? Actually, that probably makes me the moron, doesn't it? Yes. I would let you, in fact, I'm recommending it."

Sherlock considered but shook his head. "Knowing when you want to touch – that would be interesting data. How about your sight instead? You're always watching me. It can be very… overwhelming." While John considered, Sherlock retrieved a tie from the wardrobe.

Sherlock took his vital signs again, remarking, "Slightly elevated."

John deadpanned, "How surprising."

"There's a fine sheen of sweat over your upper lip, John."

"'S'been known to happen. No tickling, all right?"

Within seconds, Sherlock had him blindfolded.

Sherlock did begin at the top, stroking John's short, coarse hair. He was utterly silent for so long, John spoke up.

"Sherlock? Sherlock. You with me? How does it feel? Remember to write down how it feels."

Sherlock was lost in sensation. It felt like so many things and nothing he'd ever felt before. Straw. Grass?

"Sherlock, I'm loving that, but you have to move on. I'm a little breathless already. But remember to write down what it feels like."

"Right. Right."

He wrote: Hair. He moved to John's forehead. He wrote down smooth. "John, raise your brows." John lifted his brows in genuine surprise and Sherlock said, "Hmm." He scribbled something down. "Now furrow them."

John smiled and Sherlock scolded him. "I didn't say smile." John furrowed. Sherlock said, "Huh."

"You know you put some of those wrinkles up there, Sherlock."

"Yes, very funny."

The plan worked perfectly. Sherlock stayed in his rational forebrain and remained steady as a rock. Until, out of the corner of his eye he saw something move, and he jerked as if he'd seen a snake rearing back to strike.

John felt him and sat up in concern, "What's the matter? What's happened?"

"Your penis! It's moving! Twitching!"

"Sherlock. I told you I'd be aroused. Have you never watched yourself get hard?" he asked, bemused.

"But I'm not anywhere near your penis!"

John didn't mean to, but he raised his voice. "It's your touch on my skin. I love you and you're touching me and it's exciting, you madman!"

Sherlock was transfixed. "Well, what should I do?"

"You don't have to do anything in particular. Just what you're doing. This is about you, remember? You control the inflow of information – just ignore it if it's too much. Just keep writing everything down."

"But what about you? You're going to be frustrated."

"I'm a big boy, Sherlock. I knew what I was getting into. I can take a little frustration."

"You're not going to be angry?"

"Why would I be angry?"

"Because it's – you – I'm not taking care of it – you."

"I appreciate that, Sherlock, I really do. I'm a little curious as to why you're concerned about my comfort all of a sudden, but I do appreciate it. I'll let you know if I can't continue. In the meantime…" he trailed off.

"It's very intriguing. I knew they were capable of independent movement, but I've never actually seen it before."

"I'm happy to be your first."

"John."

"Yes, Sherlock?"

"I think I want to take care of it – you. It. Can I touch it?"

In a somewhat strangled voice, John choked out, "Please. With my blessing."

"I'm not sure what to do. Suppose I do it wrong?"

"Just don't break it and you'll be fine. If I don't like what you're doing, I'll tell you. Promise. Pretend it's yours and do what you would normally do."

Sherlock thought, then said, "I'll be right back."

John waited. He shouted, "You're coming back, Sherlock? Right?"

"Of course, don't be ridiculous." John jumped. Sherlock returned so stealthily, John hadn't realised he'd come back. He turned his head towards Sherlock's voice.

"So, I, uh, usually use a, uh, lubricant, I hope that's all right."

Sherlock's eyes opened even further when John's cock jerked and continue to fill out.

John swallowed. "Yeah, quite all right." There was a click and the bed sank as Sherlock sat. John gasped at Sherlock's first touch and realised his mistake when there was a violent lurch.

"Sherlock, it's all right, you surprised me, that's all. Keep on. It was good. Really good."

Sherlock took a deep breath. "I'm going to try again."

"Great, great." He waited.

"Okay."

"Any time now. Would be fine." And waited.

"You know. If you wanted to keep going, I mean."

"I do."

"Because I'm ready."

"Obviously."

"Unless you've changed your mind–"

"No! No, I'm just…"

John's cock was pulsing, tight, flat up against his belly.

"Sherlock."

"Yes?"
"Unto the breach."

Sherlock grabbed the lifeline.

"Once more unto the breach, dear friends, once more;
Or close the wall up with our English dead.
In peace there's nothing so becomes a man
As modest stillness and humility:
But when the blast of war blows in our ears,
Then imitate the action of the tiger;
Stiffen the sinews, summon up the blood,
Disguise fair nature with hard-favour'd rage;
Then lend the eye a terrible aspect;
Let pry through the portage of the head
Like the brass cannon; let the brow o'erwhelm it
As fearfully as doth a galled rock
O'erhang and jutty his confounded base,
Swill'd with the wild and wasteful ocean.
Now set the teeth and stretch the nostril wide,
Hold hard the breath and bend up every spirit
To his full height. On, on, you noblest English.
Whose blood is fet from fathers of war-proof!
Fathers that, like so many Alexanders,
Have in these parts from morn till even fought
And sheathed their swords for lack of argument:
Dishonour not your mothers; now attest
That those whom you call'd fathers did beget you.
Be copy now to men of grosser blood,
And teach them how to war. And you, good yeoman,
Whose limbs were made in England, show us here
The mettle of your pasture; let us swear
That you are worth your breeding; which I doubt not;
For there is none of you so mean and base,
That hath not noble lustre in your eyes.

I see you stand like greyhounds in the slips,
Straining upon the start. The game's afoot:
Follow your spirit, and upon this charge
Cry 'God for Harry, England, and Saint George!'"

Sherlock observed John's cock. "Your sinews certainly are stiffened. Henry and the bard would be pleased." In a sturdy English voice he repeated, "The game's afoot: Follow your spirit; and upon this charge, Cry 'God for Harry! England! and Saint George!"

Fortified by Shakespeare and Henry, Sherlock took a yeoman's grasp and stroked firmly, to John's pleasure. He groaned, "Most dramatic handjob of my life."

"Do be quiet, John, you're distracting me."

"Right, sorry. Can I moan a bit?"

Sherlock considered. "Quietly."

John waited, but it was difficult to tell whether Sherlock's tension and silence were a result of anxiety or arousal. "Keep narrating, Sherlock, you can't write anything down, but…"

"All right, yes, your penis is warm, warmer than your…thigh, for example." He touched as he spoke. "You're much thicker than me." Under Sherlock's attention, John was leaking profusely, apparent even through the lube, and concern ran over Sherlock's face.

"I don't…produce this much…fluid, John, is this normal?"

"Sex, Sherlock, almost everything is normal. Don't worry."

"If you're sure. You're breathing quite rapidly now."

"Yes, don't want to startle you, but I'm very close now—"

"Oh! When I'm close, I like—" Sherlock twisted his fist right up under the head of John's cock and watched in amazement as he came all over his chest. They were both breathless.

"That was…beautiful."

John removed his blindfold, hoisting himself on his elbows.

Sherlock scooped up some come, held it to his nose, then touched it with the tip of his tongue and made a face of horrified disgust. He shuddered and John laughed with oxygen he couldn't spare. "Sherlock, that's for experts."

Chest heaving, he continued. "No complaints here. It was fantastic. But how are you?" He searched his face for distress. "You look flushed. Do you need a drink? How's your head?"

Sherlock stood, turned around with his arms spread out. "I feel good! No spinning!"

Sherlock had described his reaction to the sexual attraction and emotional attachment to John as drowning in a whirlpool. It was so intense, he said, he was afraid he would be swept away. But now, he was shimmering with excitement.

He sat down and put his hand on John's foot. "I'm right here. I didn't have to leave for the Memory Village. I stayed with you the whole time."

John sat up and covered Sherlock's hand with his. He didn't even flinch. With great affection, John said, "If there were a competition for stupidest genius, you'd win. Don't you know by now? I'd never let you leave me."

They sat, fingers twined.

"So we can consider the experiment successful?"

"Not just successful, John. A breakthrough."

7

Sherlock Then

For his seventh birthday, Daddy promised Sherlock a trip into the city for a visit to The Natural History Museum. He had been begging and pestering since he had discovered the online gallery of minerals and had developed a lively email relationship with the curator of the mineral collection after Mycroft had explained that saying you were thirteen when you were six was permissible if your conversation was of a quality sufficient to convince your partner. Ms. Hansen, the curator, was sceptical, imagining that Sherlock was a graduate student pretending to be thirteen years old. The exchanges were so fascinating that she didn't mind. When Daddy contacted her regarding the possibility of a museum party for his soon to be seven-year-old, she was incredulous.

"But he's been helpful with my research – very helpful! His sample notes are better than my graduate student's. I've been having her use them as a model!"

Daddy continued texting the office. "I'm sure." Distractedly, he continued. "Oh, thank you for reminding me, he's been pestering his brother and me about a subscription to the Museum magazine. We try to keep the credit cards out of reach, I'm sure you understand, and he's asked that you reopen the online community forums. He's hoping to find someone to share samples with from the southern coast, preferably near Brighton."

By now, outside of his family, Sherlock was primarily a solitary soul. He spent as much time with Mycroft as he could, and he suffered when his confidante, mentor, and guardian left for school. Other children found Sherlock strange and incomprehensible and he found them insufferable. He generally seemed content to follow his own path and never complained of loneliness or boredom. His five cousins however, having known him from birth and having been taught to appreciate his quirks, enjoyed his company when he permitted them to. He was very good at organising search parties for scavenger hunts and laying trails in the woods, and they all looked forward to visiting. Sherlock, contrary to other social occasions, tolerated their boisterous play and with Mycroft running interference, delighted in their company, provided there was always an escape route available.

But this trip to the museum was a gala event for all of them and the anticipation had long been building. Sherlock, of course, planned to spend the outing in the mineralogy collection. He had been collecting samples he was hoping to examine with the museum's microscopes.

The cousins, on the other hand, were interested only in the dinosaurs, especially the most valuable fossil of the collection, if not in the world, Archaeopteryx, the specimen that revealed the relationship between dinosaurs and birds.

The cousins came to spend the day and then sleep over on the fifth and Mycroft kept peace. Everyone was encouraged to run madly through the woods all day in hopes that they would get a few hours' sleep. Before bed, Sherlock giggled and roughhoused with such child-like joy, that Mycroft couldn't bear to settle them down. Watching, he had a thought he was later ashamed of: he looks normal. He noted it down in his ever-present notebook. He wanted to discuss it with his father. Eventually, he read them into slumber from 'The Text-book of Petrology, Containing a Summary of the Modern Theories of Petrogenesis, a Description of the Rock-forming Minerals, and a Synopsis of the Chief Types of the Igneous Rocks and Their Distribution as Illustrated by the British Isles.' The cousins were asleep within seconds, but after twenty minutes of debate over the fissure eruption theory of the British basalts, Mycroft switched to the Brothers Grimm to get Sherlock to nod off. He began yawning immediately. The last straw was Aristotle. Mycroft quoted, "The friend of wisdom is also a friend of myth," which was an idea so convoluted that not even the brilliant seven-year-old could parse it out.

Mycroft no longer regretted the time he thought he'd wasted on reading *The Uses of Enchantment* by Bruno Bettelheim.

Mycroft anticipated the conflict during the drive. Sherlock, in his birthday clothes, was studying the Text-book and discussing specimens to see, like painite (extremely rare) and the Tissint meteorite, while the cousins spoke solely of dinosaurs. Sherlock ignored them, but the cousins politely tried to respond. "That's fascinating, Sherlock." Mostly they stared. Mycroft smiled at their attempts and tried to keep the conversation going by combining the areas of interest. "Sherlock, tell them about the type of rock fossils are found in."

Sherlock looked up from the book in irritated confusion. "Mycroft are you trying to make a joke? It's sedimentary of course. Fossils actually are stone, in reality. As the bone decomposes the minerals in the water, mostly iron and calcium carbonate, precipitate into the pores…" and he was off. Robert, the eldest, sighed, shrugged at Mycroft and returned to the discussion of T. Rex and his six-inch teeth.

When Sherlock realized he'd lost his audience, Mycroft saw the split-second look of hurt flash in his eyes and he wondered if a heart could literally break, because something in his chest hurt. Sherlock closed his book, screwed up his eyes, and exerted himself to follow the rapid-fire non-sequiturs and factoids that comprised the other children's conversation, and truly confused, he said to Mycroft, "They only like them because they're big."

Mycroft began strategising as soon as they arrived. He memorised the floor plan, especially exits and loos. He had always been a forward thinker and when it came to Sherlock's approaching strops, about-turns were highly unlikely. If he saw Sherlock becoming distressed, he planned to be ready. He also advised Daddy.

"I'm not certain, but I'm worried that we may be facing a conflict with Sherlock at the museum."

Daddy was tempted to scoff, but he trusted Mycroft's judgment on almost all Sherlock-related matters.

"Thank you for the warning, but why? He's looking forward to it tremendously. I've never seen him this excited."

"No doubt, and the cousins are too, but not for the same reasons. Do you think they'll be as fascinated with rocks as Sherlock? They're regular children. They want dinosaurs."

"Ah. I see what you mean. Is there a meeting point in the middle between them? How long might the cousins tolerate the mineral hall? How long will Sherlock last in the dinosaur hall?"

Mycroft took up the questioning. "What if we split them up? Dinosaurs first so the cousins are tired out? So that Sherlock's patience will be rewarded with the mineral hall? Take them for a snack?"

"You have your mobile?"

Mycroft resisted the urge to roll his eyes.

"Of course, Daddy. And an extra battery."

The museum was a madhouse and Mycroft and daddy exchanged worried glances. They hadn't counted on so many people and sounds echoing off high ceilings and stone walls. They had decided to visit the dinosaurs first, counting on the cousins' shorter attention spans to satisfy Sherlock's need to get to the minerals quickly. And holding it over his head might help keep his behaviour in the acceptable range. In a silent conversation, they determined Daddy would keep the cousins corralled and Mycroft would be responsible for his brother. It did not bode well that Sherlock began arguing. "Mycroft, dinosaurs are all dead, with no influence on current science. They can't contribute to the improvement of humankind, they only–"

"Yes, you are correct, and I don't disagree with you, but mainstream humans, especially the young, are fascinated by–"

"The universe is larger than they can imagine and it's expanding! And things in the universe might–"

"Certainly, but we've talked about this, Sherlock, ordinary people are…unpredictable. Inexplicable. We must make allowances."

"How long must I spend here before we can go to the mineral hall?"

"Fortunately, common people also have very short attention spans, especially– "

"How long?"

Mycroft glared at Sherlock. Usually interruptions between them went unnoticed, each leaping steps ahead at lightning speed, but even Mycroft had boundaries.

Suitably abashed, Sherlock lowered his head. "I'm sorry, Mycroft."

"An hour and a half should exhaust them. And *if* you remain unremarkable, we'll go to the minerals gallery for at least that long. Perhaps longer if Daddy promises them a snack."

Sherlock nodded knowingly. "They'll do anything for ice cream." They shared a look of confused amusement.

"So. Ninety minutes? You can share in their excitement for a bit and then, we'll find a corner for you to curl up and read in. All right?"

Sherlock nodded, as solemn as a man facing execution, but Mycroft spoiled the moment by tousling his hair.

"Maybe they'll like the moon rock. Or the Latrobe nugget? A pound and a half of gold?"

Things went well for a solid hour. Sherlock even stayed with the cousins, answering questions and correcting inaccuracies in the placards. When Mycroft saw him beginning to fidget and lose interest, he ushered him to the Images of Nature gallery, one of the quiet spaces that were helpfully listed on the website, and handed him his book.

"Only thirty minutes more, little brother. You've done so well."

Sherlock nodded, less confidently this time, but still composed. Nevertheless, Mycroft rang Daddy.

"He's getting antsy. How much longer?"

"We just have to make it to that damned archaeopteryx, but there's a bottleneck. "

"Maybe you can take him to the minerals without the other children?"

"Hmm. Maybe. But he does want to show them many of the rarer things, and he believes they'll like the moon rock, and possibly the gold, too."

"Well. There's no way we're leaving without them seeing that damned bird. Do what you can, won't you Mycroft?"

"Yes, sir. I will."

At one hour, forty-two minutes, Sherlock looked up from his book and said, "They're not coming, are they?"

"They are coming, Sherlock, Daddy promised. It's just that there's a long wait to see the archaeopteryx, that's all. We can go on ahead and they'll join us as soon as they finish."

Sherlock nodded, dejected now, and thought for a moment. "Let's go wait with them."

Mycroft was torn: pleased that Sherlock wanted to socialise, but worried about the overstimulation. "Are you sure? It's very crowded. And noisy."

"Maybe they'll be finished by the time we get there."

"The probability is very low—" but Sherlock was already heading towards the Dinosaur Gallery.

The line for the archaeopteryx was, indeed, very long and full of unhappy museum goers, and when Sherlock and Mycroft found them, Daddy was holding Rodrick, the youngest, by the hand and the rest of the cousins, like most of the other children, were fretful and bickering.

Mycroft and Daddy communicated on two levels at once, one with words and the other with glances.

"I'm very happy to see you both. Mycroft, could you head up to the front of the line to see what the estimated wait time is?" {I'm about to lose them.}

"Shall I take Sherlock with me?" {I don't know how much longer I can keep a leash on him.}

"What do you think, boyo? Would you like the exercise?" {Will he be better off here? Maybe they'll distract each other?}

It was a language Sherlock had yet to master, and so he watched with unusual intensity, even for him.

"Why don't you stay here, little brother? The crowd is rather large. You can play Twenty Questions." {The last thing he needs is more sensory input. We have to engage his brain.} Twenty Questions was a game that he could play, so long as he answered the questions. If he had to solve the mystery, it was more like Seven Questions.

Mycroft left looking over his shoulder and feeling a bit unsure of himself. This was an unusual sensation for him. He was accustomed to deliberating and deciding and moving ahead with his plan. He truly did not know what to do and thought that he and Daddy might already have lost the battle.

With many excuse mes and sorrys, Mycroft moved towards the front of the line. It was impossible to hurry through the press of people and fidgety children, some of whom had escaped their adults' grips and were milling around, running while trying not to be caught at it. He had several near misses with careening children and began wondering idly if it were easier to manage children who were rowdy and rambunctious or those who were sensitive overthinkers, when he heard a wailing that gradually increased in volume till it reached the unmistakable pitch and volume of Sherlock's call of distress.

He about-faced immediately and jogged back in the direction from which he came. His mobile rang immediately. "He headed back toward the gallery you came from. Roland spilled his grape juice on him."

Oh, god, he thought. Of all things. The worst possible

combination of sensations. The strong smell and the stickiness of the juice, the stain on his favourite shirt, and the noise and crowds, which had already taken its toll on him.

He took a sharp turn towards Images of Nature, and seeing the urgency, the security guard, who was on his radio, just pointed toward Marine Invertebrates. Sherlock had run in a straight line, and, Mycroft thought, as far as he could get from the sensory bombardment.

Mycroft found him, standing, head in a corner, holding his shirt away from his body and humming loudly and tunelessly. He started speaking from a few yards away, afraid of spooking him any further.

"Sherlock? Little brother? I know you're upset. You've tried so hard, haven't you?"

The tiniest nod and Mycroft moved closer.

"And it's your birthday. It's not fair, is it?"

The tiniest shake of the head.

"And then that sticky juice. You know what we could do? There's a shop. We could buy a t-shirt–"

Vigorous head shaking.

"Or just wear my shirt. That's fine."

Another tiny nod.

"We were frightened. We didn't know where you'd gone. And we couldn't help you. What happened?"

"I was okay, Mykie. It was loud and crowded, but I knew I could do it because I was going to see the roquesite, the first ever to bear indium." Shuddering breath.

"But then, Rolly spilled his juice, grape juice, and it was sticky and it spoiled my shirt and it smelled and my head started spinning and something was pulling me underwater and I was drowning."

He walked closer to help Sherlock take his shirt off. Mycroft saw the bony, hunched over shoulders rise and fall. "Like a whirlpool?"

Sherlock turned round, red-eyed and runny-nosed. He nodded once more.

"You're all right now. Deep breaths."

When they returned to the line, one of the security guards whispered in Daddy's ear and they were all ushered quickly through a side exit and found themselves looking into the glass case containing the fossil plate of the archaeopteryx.

"Hmm. It is interesting after all, Daddy. A dinosaur with feathers. I wonder if starlings' feathers look the same. Are feathers like fingerprints? Or are they standard between species? Or within the order? Ciconiiformes, right, Mycroft? Or is that class? Aves, the root of aviator and aviation…"

Sherlock's mind sufficiently engaged, they backtracked through the gallery at a pace that satisfied everyone. At the entrance to the Minerals gallery, Robert admonished his brothers to be polite and interested in Sherlock's lectures. "It is his birthday and it will be a present he will really love. And he was patient for us." And they were. Sherlock's excitement was contagious, and they did enjoy the moon rock and the Latrobe nugget. But the events of the day began to catch up with them all, and once Mycroft promised they'd return for a day in the Minerals gallery, even Sherlock agreed to go home.

Later at bedtime Sherlock said, "Thank you, Daddy," and laid his head in his lap. "I didn't mind the dinosaurs so very much. It was still a very happy birthday."

8

Sherlock Now

Sherlock's path forward from the breakthrough led over John's body. Once he was sure he could handle John's arousal, he explored every inch of him, gradually using more and more of his own body to do so. He allowed John tiny expansions of freedom of movement as he grew more comfortable. He let John stroke his hair. He stopped hushing his moans. And on a day John noted down in his diary, he was allowed to brush back when Sherlock's lips brushed his. Sherlock still had John stay as motionless as possible and telegraph every individual movement beforehand. Eventually, Sherlock was comfortable enough to complain that John should stop treating him like an amateur.

John decided that since the strategy of limited input had worked to increase Sherlock's comfort they would continue in the same manner, this time, with John doing the touching – but only under Sherlock's direction. He would do nothing impulsive or unexpected. John would follow directions, doing what Sherlock told him to. John was not allowed to look at him. There would be no eye contact. Sherlock made up a script – a list of what he wanted John to do, starting with Sherlock on his back. He asked John to confirm each step and wait for Sherlock's okay before moving to the next, to regulate the sensory barrage.

Sherlock's first script for John touching him:
DO NOTHING SPONTANEOUSLY AND STICK STRICTLY TO THE SCRIPT
1. Shower with tea tree soap and shampoo. No deodorant, lotion
2. Wear fleece pyjamas

3. Lie on your back, on my left side
4. Make sure your hand is warm and dry, then hold mine
5. Roll onto your side
6. Stroke up my arm
7. Scratch my scalp then run your fingers through my hair. Tug a little
8. Kneel beside me
9. Kiss: forehead, cheeks, lips (dry, without pressure)
10. Unbutton my shirt
11. I will slide my shirt off
12. Massage my shoulders
13. Remove your shirt
14. Straddle my hips without contact
15. Lay down on top of me so our chests and stomachs touch
16. As much as possible, DO NOT MOVE
17. Move down to the bottom of the bed
18. Straddle my ankles then slide your hands up my calves, thighs
19. Pending maintenance of self-regulation, you may slide your hands around to cup my buttocks
20. Pending successful completion of numbers 1-19, I will lower my trousers and pants
21. Place your hands firmly on my thighs and do not move
22. Pending sufficient arousal, I will self-stimulate to orgasm
23. Pending successful orgasm, wipe me off, lie on top of me, allow me a break.

It was a spectacular success. John's meticulous adherence to the script that first time liberated them both. They used it thereafter as a scaffold to which embellishments were added as Sherlock could tolerate them. John continued to ask permission for deviations from the protocol, adding kisses to the neck, for example, touching his stomach and chest prior to lying on top of him, or assisting with Sherlock's self-stimulation.

Sometimes Sherlock demurred or requested a delay and John obeyed every request with praise for Sherlock's courage, and reassurance that every decision he made was the perfect one. Sherlock's confidence grew. There were times when he called a halt to the proceedings entirely, but John's warm acceptance encouraged him to pick up where they had left off or try again the next day.

Sherlock's sense of ease spread from the bedroom and he began expressing his affection much more freely. He got downright cuddly and even began to initiate sexual interactions. He allowed his body to express the love he'd buried beneath.

Sherlock Then

```
Search terms: Asperger's or autism+ sleep+
initiation, maintenance, shortened, prob-
lems, disturbance, disorders; behavioural
insomnia sleep-onset type; extreme sleep
latencies; night waking; sleep-waking pat-
terns; sensory over-responsivity
```

Sherlock was born with a mortal enemy: Morpheus. Mummy was convinced he had a primal fear of never waking again, the way he fought sleep so desperately. No matter how she tried to reassure him, how overtired he was, he never went gently into that good night. Other babies took two-hour naps: his longest had been 45 minutes. It was a red-letter day.

She could sometimes soothe him into suspended animation if she left a hand resting on his back, but if she removed it before he was well and truly under, he'd pop right back up, deeply offended at her betrayal.

He fell asleep crying, in the middle of the physical act, at the injustice of having bodily needs.

Mothers with agreeable babies recommended letting him cry it out. It was an utter disaster. Two hours in and Mummy took Mycroft to the neighbours' for an emergency sleepover. Daddy took the next two, but at hour five, Sherlock vomited in his cot and the emotionally and physically exhausted parents concluded that whatever 'it' was, Sherlock was never crying it out. Despite her weariness, Mummy admired Sherlock's steadfastness in the face of his opponent, no matter who he'd decided they were. She was reassured that whoever it turned out to be, they, like she herself, could count on being soundly beaten.

Sherlock Now

It had been three weeks with no case and Sherlock's mania edged ever upwards. He was locked in a centrifugal spiral that sent him further from reality every day. He slept fewer hours each night, and John couldn't remember the last time he'd eaten more than a biscuit. Mrs Hudson left after he'd broken a second window and John was left with a whirling dervish and a chilling draft. He'd picked up some cold cases from Lestrade, tried fucking Sherlock into oblivion, but nothing held his interest for more than three minutes. "I can't shut it off! I can't make it stop!"

Out of desperation John said, "You promised you'd teach me to waltz. Nothing's coming – how about now?" He chose a polka to provoke him and Sherlock stormed over to the iPod. "Clearly that's not a waltz. This is a waltz: Brahms' A-flat Major, Opus 39."

When the music started, John stripped off his shirt, slid his hand under Sherlock's dressing gown and pulled him close. It took half an hour of swaying in ¾ time with full chest-to-chest contact before Sherlock's head was drooping. John manoeuvred him to the sofa, and laid his exhausted body down. Sherlock mumbled, "Very sneaky, Doctor." John settled in next to him, and whispered, "Major. I was a soldier, remember?"

Danke schoen, Herr Brahms.

9

Mycroft Then

Mycroft was content to lie perfectly still and observe his environment for long periods of time. A single toy could entertain him for an hour. He would examine it from every angle, map its physical qualities with exquisite precision, and explore it with almost every one of his senses (he refused to put anything other than food into his mouth). He could have written a monograph on his stuffed bumblebee, had he been able to hold a pencil. When an object finally lost its appeal, he would gently indicate that he had completed his investigation and Mummy would exchange it for another. The process would begin again, and she could count on another stretch of time uninterrupted by fussing.

When she realised that he ought to be rolling over or creeping in preparation for later crawling and walking, she pointed out the expectation to him, and he good-naturedly obliged her by mastering the skills without delay. He considered self-propulsion to be a great imposition, however. There were so many fascinating things to discover within reach, he had little impetus to move himself. In any case, he much preferred to be transported. It didn't matter how. He didn't care for being carried in arms, but he was overjoyed to be in the pram, the car, or on the back of Mummy's bicycle.

Mycroft Now

It was an average day. Gibran Lestrade woke his husband at five so they could breakfast together. A kiss at 6:00, and a long black car pulled up at the door. Mycroft stared out the window for the 20-minute drive. When he arrived, he climbed five steps and walked twenty feet to his office. For three hours he sat at his desk, dispatching operatives and authorising missions. He saw petitioners and staff members with documents that he signed, accepted, or rejected as needed. He scanned paperwork and emails until an assistant brought him cheddar scones and tea. She barred entry for the 15 minutes he allowed himself for lunch. He never left his chair.

An afternoon meeting with the prime minister of somewhere-or-other was on the schedule and he took his private lift to the rooftop helicopter pad. He spent the hour-long flight responding to the earlier emails. He crossed two borders and was met by another long black car that brought him somewhere non-descript. Intense negotiations were concluded, and his return trip was identical. Briefings completed and reports submitted, he arrived home at eleven, eyelids drooping over the curry Gi had prepared for him. Having covered a total one-hundred three yards on foot and sitting for most of the day, he collapsed into bed beside Gi, weary to the bone.

Mycroft Then

Once Mycroft was mobile, Mummy referred again to the baby books, which emphasised the urgency of 'baby-proofing' the house. According to the experts, it was "absolutely essential to examine your home from your toddler's perspective." Other mothers shared their tips, like placing dangerous items out of reach and securing furniture. The range of clever clasps and locks available were complicated enough to secure the Bank of England. The project felt completely beyond her ability. Besides, how could such upheaval be good for him?

Mummy proceeded on precedent. Mycroft wasn't like the other babies. He responded well to logic; she would explain the difference between safe and dangerous and then monitor his reactions. She described to him why he shouldn't put his fingers into electrical sockets. She told him what would happen if he touched a hot oven. She identified dangerous substances and demonstrated the consequences of falling down the stairs. It proved to be more than enough. Mycroft became a miniature insurance actuary. He took no action without assessing risk. At the playground he disapproved of reckless children: "That looks dangerous, Mummy." When in doubt, or facing a new situation, he sought adult guidance. Aside from blocking off Daddy's study and the tiled loo, the house remained unchanged and Mycroft remained unscathed. He made it through childhood with hardly a bruise.

Mycroft Now

There were colour-coded files on Mycroft's desk: green, yellow, and red. The standard, keep-the-nation-running matters went into green folders. Green projects could be handled by staff-members with sufficient clearance. Green matters were straightforward and ready for implementation.

Mycroft spent days on yellow files. The goal was always to move projects from yellow to green, to give them schedules with goals, delegated actors, and itineraries. A day spent moving projects from yellow to green meant he would eat a decent meal and get a full night's sleep. He called each evening to let Gi know when he would be home and from the tone of Mycroft's voice it was clear whether the day had gone green or red. Red days meant Gi would eat alone, at best, allowed to offer comfort or a glass of wine.

Far too often, projects moved to red. Red meant risk. Mycroft knew red would send people to their deaths. He might be saving many others, but sacrifices would be made. He held meetings, relying on intelligence collected by agents he trusted. Still. He deliberated in perfect immobility, looking distantly ahead, attempting to see into the future, juggling consequences and countermoves. His authority was such that everyone around him would bask in the glory of his successes.

For his failures, he alone would suffer the blame.

10

Sherlock Then

```
Search terms: Asperger's or autism+ senso-
rimotor+ development, behaviour; motor+ de-
lays, impairment, milestones, deficits; late
walking; crawling+ absent
```

Whereas Mycroft was happy being set down and spending time by himself, Sherlock refused to make contact with the ground. The normal baby contraptions held no appeal for him. He screamed in his cradle, he screamed in the swing, and he screamed in the car seat. If he wasn't in physical contact with another human being, he was inconsolable. As skinny as he was, eventually he became too heavy for Mummy to carry. Everyday tasks, showering, dressing, seemed to drain her of more energy than ever before.

She became increasingly anxious that Sherlock showed no signs of independent mobility.

"Will he ever walk?"

"He's perfectly capable," the doctor said. "He simply refuses. Spoiled, probably."

At her wit's end, Mummy set up afternoon practice sessions. She sat on the floor with Sherlock on her lap. Mycroft sat opposite them and tried to entice him with all sorts of tantalising objects. Nothing could induce him to marshal his efforts toward forward motion.

He finally initiated autonomous transport one afternoon when Mycroft lost patience and left him behind to play outside in the garden. In a blind rage, he launched himself from Mummy's arms and, spitting fury, he crawled across the sitting room floor and through the rear door. He skipped walking entirely and twelve days later took up sprinting. He never looked back.

Sherlock Now

It was Sherlock's fourth day on the sofa. While John expected forty-eight hours of recovery after a case, this was bordering on catatonia.

"Sherlock, did you know that astronauts suffer re-entry syndrome if they spend too long in zero gravity? If you don't stand up soon, you're going to have vertigo."

Sherlock opened his eyes so he could roll them dramatically.

"I'm resting. Don't you appreciate the tremendous effort I expended tracking down the forger?"

John rolled his eyes right back. "I appreciate. Now get up. You need a shower and I refuse to feed you on the sofa again. There are Thai dumplings here, but only once you're clean and upright."

Sherlock covered his head under the cushions and groaned.

John waved the scent of the dumplings towards him. "I'm not indulging you anymore," he said, more to himself than to his six-foot six-year-old. He walked closer, and uncovered Sherlock's head. He waved a dumpling under his patrician nose. Said nose arose and despite himself, John gave him a nibble. Then he pulled away. "Shower. Now."

"John!"

"Shower!" John said, in his Major voice, and Sherlock flung himself off the sofa. In thirteen minutes, he was back at the table, dripping and shiny, shovelling dumplings into his mouth.

Lovingly, John tousled his hair dry.

"You are a spoiled brat."

Sherlock Then

```
Search terms: Asperger's or autism+ tempera-
ment; inhibitory+ impairment, control; im-
pulsivity; response inhibition; state regu-
lation; executive+ functioning, dysfunction;
control+ interference, effortful
```

Sherlock was greased lightning. His curiosity drove him ever onward and his energy level was such that no one could keep up.

Baby proofing the house was redundant for Mycroft. For Sherlock it was impossible. He escaped from every containment system, climbed over gates, and pried locks. In three years, he had three concussions, burned off his hair, and poisoned himself. He unscrewed an outlet plate to see where the electricity lived and electrocuted himself. He had no fear and would not be persuaded by anyone else's experience. He had to see for himself. Mycroft directed him not to stick his finger into the blender blades because it would hurt. Sherlock wanted to 'investigate' and required fourteen stitches.

Everything had to be investigated.

"If Mycroft is allergic to bee stings, will I be too?" *No, even when thirteen of them sting me.*

"Why can't I use matches?" *Because I'll burn myself.*

"Why can't I eat dirt?" *Microbes will make me sick.*

Mummy was so afraid of giving him ideas, she stopped telling him things were dangerous.

He fell out of a tree, off a roof, and through the ice into the pond.

If the paediatrician hadn't been a family friend, Sherlock would have been removed from the home under suspicion of abuse. He was perennially covered in scrapes, bruises, and blisters.

Sherlock Now

Sherlock, standing between John and Lestrade, spotted the suspect first, across six lines of the underground. There were two exits from the station and Gi began shouting into his radio as he ran up the stairs on the left, John on the right. When they reached street level, John saw Gi, but not Sherlock. Panting, John yelled, "Where is he?"

"Wasn't he behind you?"

"Fuck! I'm gonna kill him."

They dodged traffic and raced down the stairs to find Sherlock, his knee in the back of a cretin who outweighed him by seventy-five pounds.

Lestrade was delighted at first. He grinned as he unclipped his handcuffs and took over. Gradually, it occurred to him to wonder how Sherlock had managed to arrive before–

"Uh-oh," he heard Sherlock mutter. Lestrade glanced up to see him looking at John, glaring daggers at him.

"Uh-oh's an understatement, mate. I'd wring your neck myself, but you're in for it anyway."

Sherlock kept his eyes on John as he turned toward Gi. "I'd be happy to come to the Yard and do the paperwork now."

Gi clapped him on the shoulder, and said, "You survived the tracks, but I don't like your chances with him." He smiled. "He's gonna kick your arse. I'll take your statement when you're allowed out to play again, you poor bastard."

Sherlock was stalling. Ordinarily he'd have swept dramatically out of the station by now, casually ignoring the officers who were swarming around the suspect. Instead, he hovered around Lestrade, supervising the arrest. Lestrade looked at him with a wry grin, which Sherlock ignored. He slid his eyes at John intermittently only to find him staring, jaws grinding, fists clenched. Waves of anger were rolling off him, almost visible, but he waited, without moving, for Sherlock to work up the nerve to face him. "John is angry."

Lestrade shook his head. "You think?" Finally, taking pity, he shoved him. "Go on then. Get it over with. It's not getting any better."

Sherlock took a deep breath and with none of his usual bravado, he walked towards John, standing by the stairs. He turned without a word and Sherlock followed him.

The silence continued in the cab. Sherlock used the time to try to formulate some kind of excuse that would soothe his husband, but it was futile. He'd broken their agreement. He had promised he wouldn't needlessly risk his life anymore.

He had braced himself for shouting, but John surprised him yet again.

Quietly, he said, "You crossed six live tracks during rush hour. The Met was everywhere. Tell me why I shouldn't be angry with you, Sherlock."

That was easy. "Because…because…"

Because I wanted to catch him myself.
Because I wanted to show off.
Because I didn't trust the NSY's abilities.
Because I wanted to see if I could.
Because I love the rush.
Because I wanted you to tell me how good I am and how proud you are of me.

Sherlock realised slowly that John would not be proud of him for doing something unnecessarily dangerous. John was always proud of him for solving cases. John always thought he was brave and clever and good because John loved him. John loved him and didn't want him to get hurt because John didn't want to lose him and – oh. John didn't want to lose him and that's why…

"You're right to be angry. I'm sorry."

"Yeah. You probably are now that you figured it out. But didn't we already figure it out? We promised to remember the thin line between having and losing each other. There were cops everywhere, Sherlock, there was no way he was escaping, but you had to be the one. I'm gonna yell and then I'm going to fuck you to make sure you're still alive and remind you what you're living for. And then I'm feeding you and putting you to bed. And tomorrow I'm gonna take out the rest of my anger on your backside."

11

Mycroft Then

Mycroft went from babbling, to single words, to two-word phrases in record-setting time. Daddy left for a month on business and when he returned, Mycroft was speaking in complete, grammatically correct sentences.

"Now that he can speak, he can learn to read," Grandmama said, and she bought him his first book. Mummy protested. "Isn't he too little for that? He might tear the pages." Grandmama scoffed. "Nonsense! He's far too clever for that." Once she had showed Mycroft the proper use of literary materials, he met her expectations. He handled paper with the utmost tenderness. His bedtime reading routine changed. He still enjoyed sitting on Mummy's lap, but insisted on holding the book and turning the pages himself. By two and a half he rejected picture books and fairy tales entirely. He showed a marked preference for non-fiction. Mummy was not convinced he was actually reading until he began selecting books without pictures for himself. His intense study of them allowed no other explanation.

Mycroft took over his own education at that point, reading any time he wasn't eating, bathing, or sleeping. He taught himself whatever he wanted to learn. Mummy tried to keep up the childhood activities. She forced him into an outing or some outdoor play each day, but, wherever they were going, he wouldn't leave without a book.

Mycroft Now

It was a state dinner and Mycroft had been preparing for weeks, calling for volumes of documents, newspapers in dozens of languages, and processing intelligence around the clock. He consumed information the way baleen whales ingested krill, sucking in terabytes of data and straining the essential out of the irrelevancies. He asked that Gi accompany him.

"Don't make me go," he protested half-heartedly.

Mycroft played on his guilt. "If you love your country or your husband, you will join me."

That evening, as Mycroft moved around the room, he spoke to the ambassadors of twenty-six countries. Gi dazzled with his fluent French and Arabic, but Mycroft chatted casually about current events, culture, and rumours, in six different languages. He knew intimate details of the lives of every guest, complimenting spouses and inquiring after children with graceful ease. His charm seemed effortless, but Gi knew it drained him. He manoeuvred Mycroft out of sight and pinched his arse.

"Ow! You know you could trigger an international crisis like that."

Gi scoffed and nibbled at his bottom lip. "You know I hate these things. Why do you make me suffer?"

Mycroft pinched him back. "To get you into a tuxedo, of course. And so I can take you out of it later."

No one, not even his husband, was immune to his blandishments.

12

Sherlock Then

Search terms: Asperger's or autism+ late
talker; rapid speech acquisition; Einstein
syndrome; Feynman, Richard; Teller, Edward;
speech or language+ formal, stereotyped,
formulaic, idiosyncratic, pedantic, didac-
tic; verbosity; vocabulary+ scripted, ad-
vanced, sophisticated; "little professor"

Sherlock was speechless. He fussed loudly and incessantly but used no consonants and uttered nothing even vaguely approaching a word. There was no doubt about his intelligence – his receptive language was highly superior when the doctor tested him. His hearing was fine. His inflections were clear enough for complaints and demands but otherwise he communicated by gesture and force of will. He insisted on being understood. Mummy would keep guessing until she hit upon his intent. Mycroft interpreted him with ease, but Sherlock was frustrated by everyone else's ignorance. Why was it so difficult for them to translate his sounds into meaning?

One cold November day in his fourth year of life, Sherlock shouted his first intelligible word, when Mummy tried to put on his mittens. "No." It remained one of his favourites.

He invented the nickname, "Mykie" some hours later, and on Christmas, composed his first sentence: "I would like to open my presents now."

He adopted complicated phrases and revelled in using them:

"According to my research…" or "After careful consideration…"

Hearing Sherlock and Mycroft speaking together was unnerving. They pontificated in a language composed of vocabulary so complex it didn't sound like English. They were so small, and their words were so large – words that no one had ever spoken aloud. In history. Like chthonic, lucubration or bombinate.

```
Search terms: Asperger's or autism+ late
bloomer; polyglot; Tammet, Daniel; twice ex-
ceptional
```

When the fears around Sherlock's lack of speech dissipated, Mummy and Daddy set out to teach the boys as many languages as they could, but it was completely unnecessary. The family had a long line of polyglots on both sides, but the speed with which Sherlock and Mycroft learned was astonishing.

They picked up vocabulary, grammar, and even accents with unconscious ease. They swallowed languages whole, absorbed them through their skin, breathed them in like oxygen. It wasn't only their ability to speak and understand; they read foreign dictionaries the way other children read comic books. Daddy bought subscriptions to international newspapers and left them lying around the house.

When they spoke to each other they would switch languages mid-conversation and never drop a syllable. They were forbidden from doing so at meals and Daddy put his foot down: English, French, or Spanish (Daddy wanted to learn), one per day.

There was a great-aunt on the Holmes' side who spoke four languages by university, but they outstripped her before adulthood. Mycroft was fluent in five by age twelve. Sherlock, even more gifted, surpassed his brother with six by age ten.

Mummy spoke to them in French, Daddy in German. They learned Russian from Grandmama, Spanish from the gardener, and Mandarin from the cook.

No one knew where Sherlock picked up Bengali.

13

Mycroft Then

Mummy so enjoyed Mycroft's company, she was reluctant to send him to school. She would miss him terribly and couldn't remember what she had done with herself before his birth. Luncheons? Charity events? She dreaded letting him go, but Daddy insisted.

She kept up a brave face. "You'll learn new things, Mycroft, and when you come home, you'll teach me all about them."

"But I don't want to go."

"You'll sing songs and play games. It will be ever so much fun. You'll make friends!"

"But I don't like singing songs. Or fun. And I don't want any friends."

Mummy already knew that.

On the first day, lips trembling, Mummy whispered, "Give us a kiss, darling. It's only a few hours."

Mycroft, tears pooling but unshed, lifted his chin and went into the classroom.

It was far worse than they had feared. The first lesson was about the colours of the rainbow and Mycroft was confused by the omission of infrared and ultraviolet. His question regarding prisms and the difference between reflection and refraction was met with silence.

Ms Simpson promptly decided to ignore him entirely.

They did, in fact, sing songs: Ladybird, Ladybird and The Itsy-Bitsy Spider. He hid behind the cubbies and wrote an essay in his notebook about urbanisation and the decline in the local population of bumblebees.

Ms Simpson explained the concept of free-play to Mycroft but she did not do a very good job, in his opinion. He decided to observe and perhaps deduce the nature of the activity.

After twenty minutes, he realised that the children in motion reminded him of the circling of electrons around nuclei. Clearly, some of the children exerted varying forces that kept the other children circling around them at corresponding speeds. Perhaps they were trying to model the elements?

"Excuse me, Ms Simpson, may I please see the periodic table?"

She stared at him blankly. "We have a sand table, Mycroft, but we only play with sand on Wednesdays."

He stared back, then added it to the list of items he'd already written in his notebook.

Things to Bring to School If I Have to Return
1. Prism
2. Calculator
3. Dictionary
4. Topographical Map
5. Periodic Table

Fortunately, Mummy had suggested he bring his magnifying lens, so for the rest of 'free-play,' he examined soil samples from different areas of the yard.

Story time was dismal; there was nothing he considered worth reading, and lunchtime disgusted him. "The other children have terrible manners. No one used a napkin!"

He enjoyed naptime. "It was the only time I could think, Mummy, they're so noisy. All day long, my head was bombinating."

The next day Mummy went to school with Mycroft, the car loaded with books and materials to keep him engaged during the day. She and Ms Simpson worked out a schedule for him. Mycroft agreed to interact with at least one other child for a half-hour, morning and afternoon. He would participate in one group activity per day. Daddy found university students who took him through primary maths and Latin that first year while the other students were mastering their ABCs and counting to one hundred. The rest of his day was spent in what everyone called 'independent projects.'

Mycroft began his lifelong study of the management of human affairs by observing the children during free-play. At first, he lured them in with new games and activities. He dictated rules that he changed as it suited him just to see how group dynamics changed. He assigned roles and had them play out complex, fascinating scenarios. Sometimes he set them against each other. No matter. They begged to be allowed to participate in his activities, and he tested strategies that eventually allowed him to manipulate their behaviour at will.

To his great relief, he was permitted to leave primary school at age seven in favour of tutors at home. He was infinite comfort and Mummy was desperate for help after Sherlock's birth.

Mycroft Now

Most of Mycroft's work was conducted in the abstract. Hands folded on his desk or under his chin, he sat perfectly still, staring into space. Occasionally his eyes would track from place to place as if watching invisible players on a stage. He spent his mornings processing information. Anonymous, interchangeable drones bustled around outside his office, but when he was ready to contemplate the momentous decisions facing him, he drew the blinds. No one was permitted to enter but Ms Barelli.

Sherlock had met her during a case and found her imperturbable. He recommended her. Once hired, she proved to be loyal, courageous, and at least half as clever as Sherlock. She learned Mycroft's patterns of reasoning and his long silences left her unruffled. She was the only person he considered capable of distinguishing the urgent from the merely important. Every issue that made its way to Mycroft himself was important, but thanks to his masterful control over his domain, very few things became urgent. Power, war, borders, diplomacy, strategy, they were all child's play to him. They were easily predicted, capitalised upon, and manipulated.

His one area of weakness was the interplay of personalities. He disliked people as a rule, but most of all he disliked their emotional decision-making, unpredictable changes in priorities, and their infuriating tendency toward irrational behaviour.

Together, Ms Barelli and Mycroft developed a technique that allowed them to compensate for his weakness in anticipating apolitical motivations. In his opinion, emotions such as jealousy or lust had no place in international politics. Nevertheless, they had a damnable tendency to arise and influence matters he considered foregone conclusions. It particularly irked him when painstakingly negotiated settlements were upended over factors having nothing to do with the issues driving the need for his involvement. He declared himself to be above ordinary and trivial passions, but in truth he just didn't allow them to factor into his decisions. The irrationality of compromising one's best long-term interests due to impulsivity was beyond a man who had toilet-trained himself at eighteen months. It was incomprehensible.

Emotions were erratic, therefore, unpredictable. He could not command what he could not understand. It was the interplay of power and strategy that Mycroft could manipulate in his head. The concepts were as visible and real to him as the pieces on a chessboard. That's where Ms Barelli's strength complemented his own.

She rummaged in the basement of a certain state building for an outdated but at-one-time essential piece of furniture: a Tactical Operations Table.

Another minor officer of the British government had once used it as a wartime plotting table, most famously during the Battle of Britain.

Ms Barelli repurposed the table and its accessories to be used as a visual display of the personal and social dynamics that sometimes blindsided Mycroft. He had only a vague understanding of the complex internal machinations of the human heart and soul. He had always preferred cold hard facts.

She found small game pieces of varied colours and shapes and used them to display the intangible motivations that frequently underlay unpredictable actions. After they designated particular pieces to represent the more volatile players on Mycroft's stages, they spent long hours discussing emotions, personality traits and motivations, to concretise the intangibles that puzzled him.

Ms Barelli used green pieces to identify love triangles held together by envy and jealousy. Grief-motivated revenge killings were represented in blue. Sometimes they switched the maps underlying the pieces when a localised situation heated up. The board changed frequently based on the classified intel to which only Ms Barelli and he were privy. They had access to the most sophisticated technology, employed it daily, but Mycroft felt privileged to use the most distinguished former official's croupier-style rake to move pieces around the table. He enjoyed manipulating the antiquated equipment, the plotters marked "F" for friendly and "H" for hostile. Quaint, perhaps, but they heralded his place in the line of descendants of the heroes of the bunker.

14

Sherlock Then

Search terms: Asperger's or autism+
lie-telling; deception; false belief; theory
of mind; ability to deceive; truth-telling;
dichotomous thinking

Sherlock's experiences in school were similar to Mycroft's. He was bored to death and astonished at the ignorance of not only the other children, but his teachers. He spent most of his time in the back of the classroom, either reading or staring off at nothing. He would appear to be a million miles away, but not so far that he didn't pipe up when someone needed correcting. He frequently made them (students mostly, but sometimes teachers) cry. During a discussion on weather, Jane stated that rain was God crying for the sins of mankind. Sherlock was outraged. "God has nothing to do with it! There is no God. When the temperature reaches the dew point, water vapour in the atmosphere condenses, then precipitates. That's where rain comes from."

Jane wept bitterly.

The visit from Santa Claus was particularly traumatic.

"But they're saying things that aren't true, Mummy! You told me it's wrong to lie. I have to tell them!"

"Sherlock, darling, you hurt their feelings when you tell them they're wrong."

"But they are wrong Mummy. You said I should treat others the way I want to be treated. If I were wrong, I would want someone to tell me. I'd want to be right. I would want to know."

And he did want to know. His curiosity was boundless.

```
Search terms: Asperger's or autism+ mind-
blindness; empathy; semantic-pragmatic dis-
order; mentalisation; pragmatic language
impairment; alexithymia
```

When Sherlock was on, he was blindingly on. He recognised patterns invisible to others. He saw the most minute changes in human behaviour and the environment, which led to deductions he had no business making as a child. He was the only person who noticed that Jamie came to school bruised every Monday morning, which coincidentally was the morning after her weekend visits with her father. The visits ended shortly thereafter. Ms Simpson was more careful after he commented that she and Ms Levy brought the same leftovers for lunch every day.

He was unnaturally alert, examining, observing, and, to everyone's chagrin, asking questions.

Ms Simpson tried in vain to teach him how to disagree politely and when comments were best kept to oneself. Everyone hoped that perhaps as he grew, he would develop some impulse control that would stop him sharing every brilliant insight he had. No one, not even Mycroft, could convince him it was worth holding back to remain on good terms with the people around him.

"You don't need to say everything you figure out, Sherlock. Everyone already knows you're clever. You don't have to prove it all the time." There was no doubt that he understood the difference between honesty and deception. It must be said he was unfailingly truthful. Unfortunately, he was also blisteringly blunt.

```
Search terms: Asperger's or autism+ food+
refusal, restriction, selectivity, avoid-
ance; limited food repertoire; high-fre-
```

```
quency single food intake; oral sensory
sensitivity; novel foods; food neophobia;
mealtime+ rituals, rigidity
```

Sherlock remained bony throughout childhood. In order to slip as much food into him as possible, the household took to leaving food in strategic places or sometimes even following him around, offering him titbits constantly. He ate so slowly, no one could stay at the table with him until he finished, and he certainly wouldn't stay there by himself. He would stay at the table until he finished if he were permitted to read and Mycroft did his homework there to keep him company.

It wasn't just the excruciating slowness with which he chewed and swallowed, but the meticulous way he arranged his food. It couldn't be mixed in any way – the salad couldn't be dressed, the gravy had to be served on the side, and none of it could touch. Any variation in flavour or texture or temperature could turn him off a food altogether and he approached anything new with extreme suspicion. The family still went out to dinner occasionally – they just didn't expect Sherlock to eat anything.

When Sherlock started school, he'd had to adjust to fixed mealtimes. Mummy was scared that he would fall further off the height-weight chart with no one to fuss over him at lunch. And he'd had to give up one of his major proteins, due to a classmate's allergy to peanut butter.

```
Search terms: Asperger's or autism+ ritu-
als, rigidity; adherence to routine; change+
resistance to, distress; visual structure;
predictability; repetition; consistency;
spontaneous environmental alterations; cog-
nitive rigidity; inflexibility; insistence on
sameness
```

Sherlock was often overwhelmed by experiences that went practically unnoticed by other children. He had a particularly hard time with changes to his routine. Mummy bought a large calendar for him, and Mycroft kept track of all of their events, trying to give him as much advance notice as possible of any deviations. Daddy's plans changed so frequently that Mycroft added a world map to the wall so that Sherlock could keep track of his location as well.

As much as possible, Ms Simpson also tried to prepare Sherlock for disruptions, as well as preparing other adults for him. She was unexpectedly absent one day and a very young, brand new teacher, Ms Danielson, was brought in. When she skipped the daily calendar activity, Sherlock interjected authoritatively, expecting her to correct the omission.

"Thank you for pointing that out to me, young man, but I think we'll just keep on. It's quite all right for us to change the schedule for the day."

It wasn't all right for Sherlock. With every change to the structure of the regular routine, he became a little more anxious and a little more distressed. Every so often, under his breath, he would say "Don't worry, it's fine. Everything will be fine." The other children watched him nervously, like he was a kettle about to boil.

```
Search terms: Asperger's or autism+ repet-
itive+ behaviours, movement, motor manner-
isms, manipulation of objects; stereotypies,
"stimming"; rocking; flapping; spinning; head
banging; pacing; perseverative
```

Sherlock rocked back and forth, legs crossed, arms clutched tightly around himself. The final straw was when the teacher refused Sherlock his rightful place as line-leader.

"Lily has been an excellent helper. She will lead."

Lily declined, having more experience with Sherlock. Lip trembling, he recalled the lessons about disagreeing politely.

"Ms Danielson, kindly examine the chart. I am the designated line leader today." Realising her mistake, Mrs. Danielson promptly blamed him. "Well, Sherlock, you haven't been an excellent helper so Lily will lead the line."

Sherlock covered his ears and chanted, "Not fair. My turn. Not fair. My turn."

Lily tugged on the teacher's sleeve, "It's Sherlock's turn. I don't want to lead the line." She even took Sherlock's hand and pulled him to the front of the line, but during their training, new teachers are advised not to change their positions, or children will see them as weak and take advantage of them.

She remained firm. "Lily, Sherlock must accept that things will not always be to his liking."

Sherlock was distraught. He wanted to kick Ms Danielson as hard as he could but knew Mycroft would be disappointed in him. He shut down completely, like a motorcar whose ignition key had been turned.

When Mummy arrived, they told her he'd spent an hour staring at the chart blankly.

Sherlock Now

It was supposed to be a day off for him, but John's mobile rang at 6:00. It was the surgery, calling to find out if he could cover a shift for a doctor who'd come down with a virus. They sounded so desperate he just couldn't refuse. He was a locum, after all. And besides, he very much wanted to go. He could use a spell with some ordinary humans, doing some ordinary things.

They had finished off a whopper of a case three days ago and Sherlock had exited his post-investigation euphoria and subsequent hibernation. Usually at this point, he wouldn't yet be bored. He would manage a few days of productive work, with a clear head, while he was still riding some of the endorphin rush from the successful, gratifying solution of a mystery. He was stable, at baseline, somewhere between ecstatic and comatose. It was such a lovely time to be with him, but it was also the safest time to leave him.

Sherlock hated the schedule to be changed for any reason, let alone at the last minute. Well, maybe he'd propose it and see what happened. How bad could it be? On second thought, this was Sherlock. In the middle of his reconsidering, in his gruff morning voice, he was interrupted by the man (manchild? ...boy?)

"You can't seriously be thinking of leaving."

Ordinarily it took a considerable explosion to rouse him. How did he know? Ridiculous question. Sherlock, that's how.

John marked every event down in Sherlock's diary, so he couldn't claim he didn't remember this one's birthday or that one's dinner party, but he never forgot John's days off.

"Problem?"

"You said you would come with me to the lab today. Are you breaking your word?"

Shit.

John scrambled for a moment. Had he promised? Or had he mentioned casually that he might accompany him? Did it matter?

"Sherlock, we've talked about this, how sometimes plans change, and–"

The fact that he sat up in the bed at six a.m. was enough of a sign of Sherlock's distress. "You said you would bring lunch because you knew I wouldn't eat once I stuck my big head into that microscope."

Shit. Did I really say that?

"Yes, I did, but–"

"You said when you could drag me away, I would have to pay you back for all the hours I made you spend in that frigid underground crypt."

Shit. I did say something like that.

"I know, Sherlock, I did, but–"

"You said that after a case I was a joy to be with."

"I don't believe I said that exactly. Besides–"

"You said when we got home, we'd take a shower to get the smell off and then you'd fuck me so hard I wouldn't be able to sit at the microscope tomorrow."

John smiled dreamily. *I definitely said that.*

He shook his head to clear it and frowned. "Yes, Sherlock, I did say that, but now I've got a chance to work. We've talked about schedules changing and how sometimes you've got to be flexible."

Sherlock whined, "John, I've planned the whole day. How am I to work if you're not there?"

"Sherlock, it's not like you pay attention to me when I come with you. You're so absorbed, I don't even think you know I'm there." He thought, *Oh god, now I'm whining.* He closed his eyes and massaged his eyebrows.

Pressing his advantage, Sherlock said, "Of course I know. You're the reason I stay so focussed!" He took the mobile out of John's hand and tugged on his shoulder to lay him back down in the bed. He rolled over and threw his leg over him, nuzzling up to murmur into his ear. "I need you there with me. Please?"

John could actually feel his resolve weakening, bending like a tree in the wind. Idly he thought of Adam and the Garden of Eden. He took a deep breath.

Buck up, soldier.

"Sherlock, there's no one else who can fill in. I've already said yes and you're just going to have to figure out how to manage without me."

Sherlock huffed and turned his back on him. "You said yes without even asking me. I thought we were supposed to discuss things before we made decisions."

Shit. John hated it when Sherlock used his own words against him. He also hated the pouting. "Come on, poppet. It's only a six-hour shift." He rolled over and spooned around him. "I won't take lunch, how's that, ten to three. You can go back to sleep until eleven o'clock! By the time you wake up and get to the lab, it'll be noon." He tickled a bit behind Sherlock's ear and kissed the back of his neck. Sherlock tried to shrug him off, but John squeezed him tighter.

"When I finish, I'll take a cab right over and you'll tell me everything you accomplished and I'll listen and be amazed and tell you how brilliant you are, I promise." He kissed him again and twirled his fingers in his hair, tugging just a little. Sherlock hummed despite himself, and softened in his arms. John smiled smugly.

"Then we'll pick up dumplings and ice cream and we'll eat it all here under the blankets."

He should have known. Sherlock hadn't relaxed; he'd slumped.

"You just want to get away from me. You're tired of me because I'm difficult to—"

John cut him off. He was familiar with this particular spiral into despair. For an overconfident mastermind, Sherlock was remarkably fragile.

"Stop it. Right now," said John as he crawled over him, cupped his face and mussed up his hair. "That's not true and it's not kind. You're trying to make me feel guilty and it's not fair." He cleared his throat meaningfully.

Sherlock opened his eyes and grimaced.

"I'm supposed to apologise now, right? Even if I don't feel sorry?"

John kissed his irresistible pouty lips, then swiped at them with his tongue.

"Yes. You are. Hurry up."

"I'm sorry if my words reveal unpleasant facts."

John pinched his arse.

"Ow, all right I'm sorry. I shouldn't have said that." Still pouting, he said, "The kind with nuts and marshmallow bits?"

"I'll feed it to you, one spoonful at a time. You can suck all the ice cream off…" John grabbed his lip between his teeth and pulled gently. "…and I'll eat the chewy parts you don't like…" He nibbled his top lip this time. "… right out of your mouth. Like this." He licked at his tongue, chasing imaginary almonds and marshmallow bits.

Sherlock Now

Food with stipulations:
- Swordfish and tuna, but no other fish
- Peanut butter without peanuts
- Salted butter only
- Whole milk or semi-skimmed; not one percent

Food he doesn't like:
- Tomatoes (Seeds, skin and slimy parts. He likes the pale, meaty parts. Sometimes John cuts it up for him.)
- Mint and chocolate together
- White chocolate on principle. Contains no chocolate.
- Red pimientos in green olives. (Sometimes John plucks them out so he can eat just the olives.)
- Ice cream with too many things in it. (Sometimes John eats all the things leaving the ice cream. Once Sherlock sucked the ice cream off all the nuts and marshmallow bits and let John take them right out of his mouth. They got halfway through the pint. When they were finished doing other things it had melted. John ate it anyway. He said he needed to restore his strength.)
- Grapefruits
- Sweet and sour sauce
- Really, anything that's sweet and sour at the same time
- Vanilla ice cream with vanilla bean in it. John didn't believe he could taste the bean, but they conducted a blind taste test and John happily paid up with a blowjob

Food that gives him migraine:
- Red wine (more than one glass)
- Hazelnut coffee
- Chinese food with monosodium glutamate in it (Sherlock always forgets to ask. John always remembers.)
- Cheese, especially blue

Food Sherlock hates:
- Cucumbers (The slimy seeds, and rind. He'll eat the white meaty parts. Sometimes John cuts it up for him.)
- Blueberries (tiny seeds inside)
- Cranberries (see above)
- Kiwis (see above plus slimy and hairy. He'll eat strawberries. The seeds are outside. John doesn't understand that one.)
- Canned fruit in syrup (Once John sucked the syrup off and Sherlock ate the fruit right out of his mouth. Sherlock fell asleep after they finished the other things so John ate the rest in peace.)
- Celery with strings. John chops it up very small.
- Margaritas with salt
- Vinegar on crisps
- Really, anything that's sour and salty together

Food that has made him gag:
- Okra
- Kidney beans
- Mushrooms
- Pizza with pineapple on it
- Chocolate covered pretzels
- Really, anything that's sweet and salty together
- Anchovies
- Sardines (still in the can)
- Yogurt ("Spoiled milk.")

Food that shouldn't even be considered food because it's made him vomit. As in running from the table, barely making it to the loo in time:
- Mint jelly
- Kidneys
- Oysters
- Liverwurst
- Pâté (At a state dinner that took Mycroft weeks to arrange. Fortunately, Sherlock identified the double agent prior

to the gastric eruption. John held the hair away from his forehead while he vomited. Sherlock wanted to include that in his wedding vows but Lestrade talked him out of it.)

- Bologna

Sherlock Now

Sherlock adored John's cock. It was thick and ruddy, transitioning to an angry purple at its peak tumescence. It had been a little frightening when he'd seen it first and once he'd had the courage to wrap his hand around it, he couldn't imagine it fitting anywhere else.

It had taken some time, but it turned out to fit perfectly everywhere Sherlock wanted it to go. He loved it in his mouth. He loved licking it, sucking and suckling at it, swirling his tongue around it and sliding it down his throat. Once they had figured it out, he loved it in his arse too. John said no one ever loved it better.

But now Sherlock lay on the bed, his legs dangling off, hands covering his eyes. He was upset and wailing, "I just can't!" He couldn't bear the taste of John's come. John sacrificed meat, dairy, alcohol, and caffeine (for no one else but Sherlock). He had tried pineapple juice, cranberry juice, gallons of water, parsley, lemon and peppermint, plums, kiwis, blueberries, cranberries, celery, and in the most humiliating purchase of his life, Yummy Cum Semen Flavour Enhancer (for no one else but Sherlock).

Sherlock could take in his entire length and swallow around it, but the taste of his ejaculate made him gag. Nothing overcame the salty bitterness.

"Sherlock, stop it. You're focused on the wrong elements of this experience. It's not a transaction. Just because I do something doesn't mean you're obligated to. I ate scorpions and rancid camel butter in Afghanistan. You won't eat custard! Do I look disappointed? Dissatisfied in any way? I'm completely sated. Drunk with pleasure. You've left me practically unconscious. I couldn't even tell the difference. Well done you."

Sherlock whined anyway. "But I want to! It's a weakness I should be able to overcome."

"Don't be ridiculous! You can't help it."

"But John, you make me feel…ugh…precious to you when you swallow….my…fluid."

John kissed him and said, "You can call it come, posh boy."

Sherlock pouted and as he did so often, John relented. "Sorry, sunbeam. I was not teasing you. Although I was. And, good, I'm glad you feel that way. You are precious." Another kiss. "But I don't feel not precious because you can't stand the taste. How about this: pretend tests reveal you have an allergy to semen. And shellfish. Doctor's orders: no more clams and pull off before I come, to prevent anaphylactic shock."

Sherlock tried to pout and smile simultaneously. "Fool."

John pulled him back up on the bed and snuggled him, big spoon despite the many-inches deficit. "Your fool."

John declared a moratorium on blowjobs.

Sherlock persisted in his attempt to overcome his perceived inadequacy despite John's prohibition. "There's got to be a way. I will figure it out." Sherlock chewed ice cubes, but it turned out to be counterproductive to the ultimate goal. He numbed his tongue with dental anaesthetic, but it interfered with his technique and numbed John as well. He surreptitiously collected samples and tried to acclimate himself to the taste. When John asked about the jars in the fridge, Sherlock tried lying, but John wasn't fooled. He shouted and refused to cooperate. He forbade any further experimentation.

Sherlock set the mental machine to work on the problem in the background so as not to irritate his love.

During flu season, Sherlock came down with a sore throat and milked it for all it was worth. He played on John's caretaking instincts, lounging on the sofa, whimpering piteously and demanding constant attention. John fed him up with rich soups and ice cream. He sat behind him, holding up his head so he could drink John's 'miracle remedy.' John stroked and coddled, long after he was certain that the virus had run its course, trying not to let on that he was enjoying it. So long as he was fussed over, Sherlock was biddable and cuddly, and it was a pleasure for them both.

Gi called with a case and Sherlock wouldn't pretend he needed nursing anymore. He loved the miracle remedy, and wanted to make more, but John said, "No, you'll figure out the ingredients and you'll never drink it again. I know you."

"Give me some credit, John. I am a grown up."

"In theory. But you won't believe me anyway. It's hot water, honey, cinnamon, and apple cider vinegar. You should hate it."

That look came over Sherlock's face, the staring, I've gone somewhere else look, that said he was on the edge of some remarkable realisation.

"Why don't I?"

"I imagine you love the honey so much it masks the vinegar. And so long as you didn't know what it was, you allowed yourself to enjoy it." John was quite smug about it.

The excitement on Sherlock's face was lovely. "Tonight, John. Oral sex."

"Wha – we talked about this, Sherlock, experiments on me are off. I've done everything you've asked including that ridiculous Yummy–"

"It's not on you this time! It's on me! Or rather my taste buds. Please, John, I promise not to get upset if it doesn't work. But you have to let me try. And this time you might actually like it. If I can't solve a problem like this, there's really no point to being brilliant."

That evening, John established parameters: No mechanical devices or equipment including receptacles of any kind, no pharmacological substances and no bodily modifications.

Sherlock grinned mischievously and said, "Not only will you approve this time, John, you'll be enthusiastic! It involves increased calories. For me! And I'm going to go shopping!"

"Where? No hardware stores, no—"

Holding up his hands, Sherlock said, "The supermarket. Nothing dangerous. May get a little sticky, though."

John put his hand on Sherlock's forehead. "Are you sure you're not ill again?"

Sherlock shook it off and snorted.

John laughed and grabbed him around the waist. "Perhaps you haven't noticed, but our sex is usually sticky, Sherlock. No objections to food on my – your part."

"Excellent! I think there's still some pineapple–" John threw a pillow at him.

"Out! Before I change my mind."

Sherlock came back an hour later with one full sack and refused to allow John to look inside them.

John was curious and intrigued. They tried to have dinner. John tried to have dinner. Sherlock was far too excited and ate just as much as he knew it would take for John to be satisfied. And he ate it in three minutes. He spent the rest of John's meal trying to get him to finish. John ate placidly, impervious to Sherlock's bullying.

John was a little nervous about the rest of the evening's events and kept taking sidelong glances at the grocery bags that Sherlock had left on the counter. He refused to allow his mind to wander over what might be in them.

When he finished the meal, he asked, "Would you like afters?"

"Ha! Yes! Most decidedly so! But not at the table tonight, John," Sherlock said. He flourished himself from the table and grabbed John by the hand. Sherlock picked up the bag and swirled both of them to the bedroom.

"Now John, in order for this to be a valid experi – what I mean to say is that, in order to maintain my focus, I need you to follow my directions precisely." More timidly, he asked, "Is that okay?"

John gave him his very sternest look and said, "So long as you tell me what you're going to do first. I don't want any surprises."

Sherlock grinned, his confidence back, and held his hand over his heart. "I promise. Now, take off your clothes and lie down." While John complied, Sherlock pulled the duvet off the bed and covered the bed with a few towels.

John smirked. "Planning on making a mess, are you?"

Sherlock reached into the bag and took out a glass jar and 2 plastic bottles.

Sherlock resisted many childhood activities, such as finger-painting, making mud-pies, and playing with clay. He hated getting his hands sticky. He resisted feeding himself, and if he got anything on his hands, he would whine and hold them up to be cleaned immediately.

He had no such reservations after he dripped chocolate sauce in a thin line straight down the centre of John's chest, over his navel and right down to the edge of where the darker wiry curls began below.

"Now, John, if you don't want to end up sticky, you need to hold still. I need to be able to get–" He began licking. "–every–" Another lick. "–drop." Sherlock lifted his head and grinned up at him. John grinned back.

"Be careful. Wouldn't want you to miss any."

Sherlock dribbled another line, beginning at his left nipple, crossing his breastbone and ending with a little puddle covering the right. John inhaled deeply when Sherlock drew his flattened tongue over that right nipple, but he looked up sadly and said, "I missed some. I'll have to take another pass over it." He did. "Got it. Perhaps I'll try a different strategy on the left. Smaller strokes this time."

The tiny kitten licks had that nipple stiffening right up and John doing his best to keep breathing.

Sherlock was very thorough, switching the chocolate sauce for jam and honey and trying different types of licking, dabbing, and lapping. John's cock had taken a noticeable interest in Sherlock's tongue and Sherlock had noticed John's cock. "I think my technique has improved, John, wouldn't you say? And in favour of my theory, you seem to be sweating a bit, but the sweetness of the chocolate is masking the saltiness almost completely." Sherlock reached down and stroked John to fullness. "I believe we're ready for testing. Do you concur?"

Finding it difficult to speak, John nodded. "Of the three, the honey overwhelms my palate most completely, so if you have no objections…" John shook his head vigorously and Sherlock proceeded to drip thin spirals of the golden syrup around the crown of his cock. He slid his lips over the head and hummed. "This is very promising, John. I taste none of the usual sharpness. I'll have to make sure the honey is all over before the bitterness intrudes." John propped himself up on his elbows to watch his love drip the honey all the way up and down and around his fully engorged self. "I've done a bit of research on the supposed map of the tongue. No such thing. Bitterness and sweetness can be detected by every taste bud."

Sherlock dove down as far as he could without gagging. He sucked as much of the honey off as he could and pulled off at the top to replace it. John had a fleeting thought that if he were in a more rational state of mind, he might be concerned about the viscous puddle under his arse, but he remembered his earlier words to Sherlock and refocused on the exquisite sensations he was wringing out of him. He was, he admitted to himself, quite interested in the outcome of the experiment. He was truthful when he said he didn't care about the swallowing. It was more of an intellectual curiosity now. He knew how smug Sherlock would be if he were to achieve his objective and then John would get to tell him how smart he was and Sherlock would blush and John lost his train of thought completely as Sherlock sucked and licked at the same time.

He popped off again and reapplied the honey, licking his lips and humming as he licked up a drip of honey/precome mixture that fell from the leaking slit onto John's belly. He poured some more onto his finger and smeared it onto his lips, then reached up and kissed him. When he lifted his head, he said "Sweetness, John. Sweetness and nothing but."

John groaned at Sherlock's now steady rhythm. He slid up and down, the thick honey and Sherlock's saliva creating a unique lubricant on John's throbbing cock.

John got closer and closer, torn between letting his head drop back and staring at Sherlock, whose mouth and chin were covered in stickiness. It was obscene in the most agonisingly delicious way, no pun intended. Panting now, and his orgasm about to overtake him, he tried to warn Sherlock, to give him time to pull off at the last minute. If it's possible to scowl at someone while giving a blowjob, Sherlock scowled. He pulled off to add more honey and John groaned in complaint. Sherlock began, "John, perhaps you've forgotten. Scientific—"

John growled, with his last remain breaths, "Shut up, Sherlock! Finish or I'll smack your arse—" Sherlock took a swig from the bottle and John interrupted himself with a groan as Sherlock resumed the procedure. Fortunately, the interruption didn't interfere with John's flow and the critical juncture of the experiment was reached without delay. Sherlock held John as deep in his throat as he could, hoping to bypass his taste buds entirely. He swallowed. He swallowed all of it and smiled up at his love with satisfaction, as smug as John imagined he'd be.

Hoarse and wheezing, John mumbled, "Bravo."

15

Sherlock Then

Search terms: Asperger's or autism+ sensory+
integration, processing, stimuli, perceptu-
al experiences, resistance, heightened response, atypical response, modulation, ori-
ented behaviours, correlates to temperament;
overreactive; self-regulation; regulation
disorders; arousal modulation

When school wasn't mind-numbingly boring, it was a swirling confusion of new and uncontrollable sensory input. It left Sherlock dizzy and hyper-stimulated. He frequently complained of headaches and usually took a nap after school. Once, on the very first cold day in October, he went missing for thirty minutes. They found him in the wardrobe, coat over his head, rocking back and forth. He hadn't responded to his name being called because he was humming, fingers stuck tightly in his ears. When Ms Simpson asked him why, he said the noise from the radiators was crawling around in his head. No one else had noticed. The custodian, a sullen, solitary man, explained to him how the boiler worked and that soothed him somehow.

He couldn't find words to express the sensations he experienced. Strangers thought he was lying or possibly hallucinating.

No one knew how to make it better. The bells that marked each period made purple and green sparks glitter behind his eyelids. The fluorescent lights whooshed at him like the seashells that Mycroft held to his ears. He dreaded the roaring sound of the students in the cafeteria – a sour, bitter, yogurt-y taste flooded his mouth and nauseated him to the degree that he couldn't eat the only lunch he would agree to at the time: a single banana.

```
Search terms: Asperger's or autism+ synaes-
thesia; synesthesia; perfect pitch; savant;
heightened sensory sensitivity; hyper-atten-
tion to detail; detail perception
```

One day during Year Five, Mycroft asked Sherlock about his day.

"Uninspiring."

Mycroft hummed sadly, commiserating.

"Except the bells sounded purple and red today, not purple and green. Do your bells sound purple too? Do they sound like two colours together like mine? Do they sound the same colour every day? Or do they change? Mine never changed before. Will they change every day now?"

Mycroft stared at him, and laid his hand against his forehead to feel for fever. Twice before, high temperatures had sent Sherlock into delirium. No fever. He was quite used to Sherlock's questions stringing out like silk from a spider, but no matter how long the thread, the questions spun out in logical progression. These were nonsensical.

Mycroft grabbed Sherlock's head between his hands and looked into his eyes: pupils equal. He covered his eyelids gently for a moment and released them: reactive. "Did you hit your head at school today, Sherlock?"

Concussion? Seizure?

Sherlock wriggled and batted Mycroft's hands away, glaring at him. "Stop touching me! I didn't hit my head! I asked you a question! Why won't you answer me?" He clenched his little fists and stomped.

Mycroft frowned. "You asked me five questions and I'm not

answering them because they don't make any sense, Sherlock. Can you see clearly? Is your vision blurry?"

Heading for a strop, Sherlock shouted. "I can see fine. Besides, I told you, it was the sounds that had the colours."

Mycroft, as always, remained calm and logical. "Sounds don't have colour, Sherlock. You hear sounds. You know that."

Sherlock crossed his arms and pouted. "I know you hear them. But I see them too. And today they changed. Today they were purple and red. I thought maybe you could see them too. I'm not lying! You believe me, right, Mykie?"

Mycroft bent down to him, even more anxious, and stroked his fingers through Sherlock's silky hair. "Of course, I believe you." He did. "Do you see colours for other sounds too?"

Mollified, Sherlock answered brightly, "At lunchtime the cafeteria sounds grey like thunder. And the fire alarm is red. But the kettle is more brownish."

"And you see these colours all the time? Or just recently?"

Sherlock was matter-of-fact. "All the time. It's, just, today, the bells changed."

Mycroft hadn't given up on his concussion theory and wanted Sherlock still, just in case.

"Will you be good for me and go have a lie down in your bed? I'll bring you biscuits and milk, if you'll go wait for me there. Are you sure your head doesn't hurt?"

"Biscuits?" He took off running. "I'll lie in bed for biscuits!"

Mycroft briefly thought of speaking to Mummy and asking if she could take Sherlock to the doctor, but felt that might do more harm than good. He called his father.

"I know you're working, Daddy, but I think there's something wrong with Sherlock. I don't want to make Mummy ner – well, upset her, but he might need Dr. F."

"There's a good lad, Mycroft, calling me instead of troubling your mother. And good looking out for the little man. Tell me."

"He's not making sense. He's talking about the colours of the school bells and fire alarms, that they're purple and green. And asking me what colour mine are. He doesn't have a fever and he says he hasn't hit his head."

Daddy considered. "From what you've said, I think he might have a condition your uncle had too. It's called synaesthesia – when a person sees colours as they hear sounds or music. Your uncle had colours that were attached to numbers and letters. It's rare but not an illness. You keep him in bed till I get home and make sure he's not acting any more quirky than usual, but I'm almost certain it's just another of his gifts. Another way he's unique. And lucky to have such a brilliant big brother watching over him. Well done, son."

Mycroft beamed.

After the purple bells, everyone realised that Sherlock was subjected to twice as much sensory stimulation as the other children: sounds had colours, smells made noise; he could hardly explain his physical experiences and he stopped trying. Mycroft and Mummy interceded for him.

Mummy sent an extra heavy quilt to school. Wrapped around his shoulders, the weight of it helped to calm him down. She convinced Ms Simpson to give up asking him to sit still. Sometimes he could attend to a lesson if he were permitted to pace back and forth at the rear of the classroom.

Mycroft made sure to put a little of Daddy's aftershave on each of them in the morning. When Sherlock felt overwhelmed or there were smells he couldn't tolerate, he would tuck his nose inside his buttons to comfort himself with the familiar scent. Mycroft visited his classroom and suggested cutting the harshness of the fluorescent bulbs with pastel-coloured cloths.

Ms Simpson made him up a quiet spot inside a play tent where he could retreat when it all got too much. Her clever suggestion of big pillowy headphones helped muffle the sound of a hundred children socialising over their lunch breaks. They were so large, sitting at the top of his thin frame, he looked as though he'd overbalance in a stiff breeze.

Sherlock Now

Sherlock was a violinist. He had perfect pitch. He could read and write music, play by ear and improvise. He had memorised hundreds of pieces and of all his possessions, held his violin closest to his heart. But there were times that he clutched it, and sawed the same notes over and over, walking back and forth for hours. John left the flat when he got into one of those patterns.

Sometimes he paced, passing a pencil between his fingers or gesticulating, in a silent, animated conversation.

There were other behaviours that put him in a trance-like state. He would endlessly spin a coin on the table, watching it slow and fall. He would try to balance a glass on its edge or twist a piece of his hair.

John tried not to interrupt him when he was engrossed in this seemingly meaningless activity. He came to like a man waking from a coma: disorientated, slow, and fuzzy. He had to be eased back into consciousness. Doctor Watson might have been concerned that he'd had a seizure, but the motions never ceased. These episodes were different from the deep thinking that sent Sherlock to staring off with steepled fingers. Those were purposeful. These altered states were directionless.

No matter how many times he was asked, Sherlock couldn't say where he'd been.

Sherlock's body annoyed him endlessly, even useful bits like fingers and legs. Ridiculous looking noses served a purpose. Somewhat vain, he felt conflicted about his hair, but the appendix? Gall bladder? The spleen! When Sherlock maligned nipples, John drew the line. It was early in their physical relationship, and while John was still the admitted expert, Sherlock scoffed.

"The male nipple is pointless! An evolutionary dead end, John! You're a doctor!"

"You'll get no argument from me on the appendix, Sherlock. I removed two in the field, one from a little Afghani boy. Wicked, nasty things. Killers. You can live a long, happy life without a gallbladder. Wouldn't give up a spleen without a bit of a fight, but it'd be a mistake letting go of those nips, no matter how testosterone-poisoned you were."

As with many, genius or no, Sherlock did not know what he didn't know, and he scoffed at John's extensive but underappreciated expertise. John threw down the gauntlet. He proposed fifteen minutes, but Sherlock recklessly offered thirty. John smiled mildly, confident as he'd ever been. They set terms. Sherlock would lie on his back, perfectly still. His penis was off-limits. Sherlock would determine when the contest was over. He only lost if he conceded before the 30 minutes were up.

John set to work professionally and businesslike.

He set his timer and looked down at his love, spread out for miles on the bed, his arms extended over his head.

"You might want to reconsider your position, Sherlock. You're going to be even more sensitive with your skin stretched out like that."

Arrogance dripping from his voice, Sherlock asked, "Surely you shouldn't be stalling, John. I can withstand anything for thirty minutes and I'm sure you've wasted at least one of them already."

"I'm really going to enjoy this. I'm not even going to make you hold still. Wriggle as much as you like."

Sherlock snorted. "I've never wriggled in my life."

Under his breath, John said, "I have video."

Even further under, Sherlock said, "I erased it."

John stretched Sherlock's hands gently to the side and began with the anatomical landmarks of the chest. He touched "the angle of Louis, which marks the splitting of the trachea into the right and left lungs. Yours," John helpfully noted, "are rising and falling more rapidly than a moment ago."

"It's also useful for locating the ribs," which John counted carefully with gentle fingers, trying not to tickle. "On the anterior surface of the chest, here," sliding over them slowly as he spoke, "on the pectoral fascia and pectoralis major muscles, between the second and sixth ribs, lies the breast."

John covered each of them with his hands and squeezed gently and repeatedly. "We all start as female in utero, Sherlock. Breasts and nipples are standard issue. They're present before testosterone appears. And since they don't cost anything, they haven't been selected for elimination evolution-wise."

He applied a little friction with his palms, and traced the muscles, "Subclavius major subscapularis, coracobrachialus, serratus anterior," and, counting again, "The distinctive breast tissue extends from the second–" he palpated with his fingertips "–to the sixth–" and continued his lecture.

"Anatomically, the nipple helps to quickly locate the fourth rib, although yours, Sherlock, falls directly above as opposed to slightly below as in most males. Let me show you." He let his fingers tap like raindrops over them and hummed when they took notice. "They sit vertically below the centre of the clavicle. Yours are particularly prominent." John drew his tongue from the tip of each of them to the sternal notch in turn. He covered each with his tongue, just letting it rest there, warm and wet, for a few moments. He blew on them gently. "The cool air makes them stand up – same mechanism as goosepimples." He circled around them, flicked, nibbled, stroked, and with every move, Sherlock's tension ratcheted up another notch.

John planned to make him beg.

Sherlock tried desperately to quash his rising arousal by using his adolescent strategies. He recited the atomic weights of the elements alphabetically and then by size. He conjugated Aramaic. He thought of Mycroft. But this sensation, he'd never even imagined. Surely, his fingertips had more nerve endings than his nipples. They'd never tingled like this.

The more John licked and sucked, the more Sherlock throbbed. He kept driving his mind away from the stimulation, but then John would change strategy. *What is he doing with his lips?* And he was right back there, fixated on the ridiculously tiny points of flesh. It was a scientific problem similar to hundreds of others: How does this tiny source of input generate such enormous output? And like light itself, how did the energy transfer itself so quickly from one place to another? How could his nipple be wired directly to his cock?

When John really set to work pulling gently and then taking the sensitised bits of skin between his teeth, Sherlock saw defeat stalking him. He flailed, trying to find something to distract himself from the electricity pulsing from his chest. Finally, he acknowledged that he couldn't escape and threw himself headlong into the pool of pleasure waiting for him. Sherlock took his loss in exquisite and loose-limbed humour, letting bygones be bygones.

16

Sherlock Then

Search terms: Asperger's or autism+ emotion-
al+ intensity, distress, reactivity, dys-
regulation; inappropriate behavioural reactions; maladaptive behaviour; perseveration;
affect regulation

After Mycroft shared some independent research he'd done on children and school transitions, Ms Simpson felt better prepared to help Sherlock adjust. She understood his intellectual needs and hoped to help him develop social skills based on her success with Mycroft. She had a much broader notion of what acceptable classroom behaviour was by the time of Sherlock's enrolment.

Thanks to her encouragement, his classmates did invite Sherlock to play. His vivid imagination and adult manner captivated them, and they allowed him to direct them in elaborate playacting scenes, some factual, some imaginary. But he refused to join in the traditional childhood games. He resisted taking turns or showing team-spirit and never had been as even-tempered as his brother. He was unable to shake off the minor sorrows of childhood. He could not forget, and it left him unable to forgive. He couldn't move on.

Any type of competition was fraught. He knew far in advance whether he could win or not and hated losing so much he would walk away rather than play to the end. The first time he lost a game of chance, he banged his head on the floor so hard he made himself woozy. "No, no, it's not fair! I was the closest! I tried to spin a six!" He wept inconsolably for forty-five minutes, brokenhearted.

When Sherlock's sobs died down, he curled up in a corner, sucking his thumb. Ms Simpson tried to soothe him, but he didn't respond. Mummy was called but she knew her limitations when it came to Sherlock's 'moods.' She often increased his agitation, despite her best efforts. She picked up Mycroft first.

When they arrived, Mycroft looked at no one but his baby brother and walked slowly to him, without a word. First, he just sat next to him without moving. Then he laid a single hand on his shoulder. He left the hand there for a few minutes, then shuffled closer so that he was flush against Sherlock's back. Gingerly he started to rub his arm and finally, finally Sherlock rolled over and buried his face in his brother's lap, crying again, but softly now, taking deep shuddering breaths. After a while, Mycroft pulled him up against his chest and rocked him back and forth. The process took twenty minutes and was conducted in complete silence. Eventually, Mycroft leaned down and whispered into Sherlock's ear. He nodded and Mycroft helped him to his feet. They left the classroom together. Mummy apologised to Ms Simpson and Sherlock stayed in his room for two days, until Daddy got home.

"Where's my boyo?" He lured him out with a new pair of binoculars.

```
Search terms: Asperger's or autism+ affect+
reduced, flat; emotional blunting; detach-
ment+ emotional, social; facial+ expressivi-
ty, expression
```

Mycroft understood Sherlock's thinking and to a certain degree, his feelings of frustration and grief. He did not understand why he allowed things to affect him so deeply and for so long. No matter how many times Mycroft explained about separating his thoughts from his feelings or using the former to control the latter, Sherlock could not. Once his feelings overwhelmed him and he had started a strop, he was incapable of interrupting or redirecting it. It ended only when he'd worn himself out and collapsed in exhaustion. Afterwards, he was as baffled as everyone else as to how things had escalated so quickly and drastically.

Mummy tried to arrange play therapy for him at Ms Simpson's urging, but after a breakdown in a session, the therapist recommended medication and that was the end of that. Everyone was appalled at the idea. Sherlock was troublesome and trying. But he was also perfect – as in perfectly himself. He would not be swayed by other people's opinions. His intensity was difficult to manage, for sure, but wasn't he entitled to his passion and determination? Should he be medicated out of his identity? Or raw brilliance?

Sherlock refused to engage with any other therapists and the idea was given up. He began a lifelong struggle to push his feelings down and keep them buried.

```
Search terms: Asperger's or autism+ memo-
ry+ superior, enhanced, rote, synaesthesia,
savant
```

Once the idea of therapy was abandoned, Mycroft stepped up again and made new rules for Sherlock, explaining that they would make his life easier at school with the other children.

No more win-lose games, only polite correcting of people's mistakes, and save all questions to ask Mycroft, Daddy, or Mummy at home. And then Mycroft taught him the Method of Loci, or as Sherlock came to call it, the Memory Village. Mycroft explained that the ancient Romans could remember very long speeches by attaching chunks of material to places and objects in their rooms. Then when they wanted to remember something, they would take an imaginary walk around the room, look at the objects that were there, and see the attached memories.

"Do you see, Sherlock? Now you can remember anything you want to remember by putting it in the places in your room! And when Ms Simpson or the children are boring, you can just find new things to put into your Roman room, or wander around remembering things, or even tidy up!"

"But Mykie, there are too many things to fit in my room! I want to remember everything important!"

"Well, silly, where's your room?"

The little boy thought, then smiled. Mycroft savoured it – at that time in Sherlock's life, the smiles had been few and far between.

"In our house. Can I use the whole house?"

"Silly again – you can use as many houses as you like. The summer house, Grandmama's house – the whole village! London, even England, if you have enough things to remember."

"I'm still little. Maybe just the village now. Can I go outside too, or do I have to stay inside the houses? Because I know every tree in the beech copse. And all the stones by the brook. Can I hide things under the stones?" He leaned forward conspiratorially. "I've already hidden some real things under them."

Mycroft felt ridiculously pleased that Sherlock trusted him enough to tell him so. "Of course."

"But someday I'll need all of England."

"You certainly will. You're going to have so many things to remember, little brother. You've learned so much and you've barely started school." Had any of it been helpful? "For now, the village might be enough. You'll have to learn it very well, every house, all the secret corners. The more details you build into your mental map, the more things you'll be able to remember." Mycroft bent down and whispered to him. "Can you keep a secret?"

Sherlock's eyes opened saucer-wide. He nodded solemnly.

"I use a palace. Guess which one."

Sherlock whispered back, "Which one?"

Mycroft cupped the little boy's ear. "Buckingham."

```
Search terms: Asperger's or autism+ inter-
ests+ repetitive, circumscribed, intense,
specific, narrow, focused, idiosyncratic,
restrictive, special; systemizing; hypersys-
temising; attention to detail
```

School improved for everyone eventually. Sherlock brought as many books from home as he could carry and everyone agreed, if he didn't make anyone cry, he could use the upper grade library on Fridays. Whenever he found subjects of interest, he immersed himself with a religious fervour that would have impressed Saint Augustine. New fascinations thrilled Mummy because it meant she could bring him to the library where he could pester the librarians and she could take a break.

He was permitted to lecture the class once a week on areas of his expertise. Mycroft helped him to translate the talks into language the children might be able to understand, and Sherlock relished the praise Ms Simpson gave him. Thanks to her patience and persistence, he learned to share his microscope to a certain degree. He spent an hour each day in the Memory Village and everyone left him alone during that time. (Once he entered, he was unreachable anyway.) Most of the time he was still motionless, but sometimes he paced back and forth or laughed to himself, but the other children ignored him the way he ignored them. Unfamiliar adults would always be problematic.

Sherlock had none of Mycroft's interest in controlling his peers and considered them at best an annoying distraction.

In general, they left each other baffled.

Things Sherlock Became an Expert in in Primary School
- Lorries and construction equipment
- Pirates

- Trains, train lines, and train schedules
- The Underground
- Reptiles, especially venomous ones
- Spiders, especially venomous ones
- Plants, especially poisonous ones
- Venoms and poisons, especially – never mind
- Maps, especially London
- Airplanes, airports, and air routes
- Cryptography
- International currency
- The skeletal system
- Meteorology and weather patterns
- Bees

Things Sherlock Became an Expert in in Secondary School
- The Periodic Table
- The history of weaponry
- The torture and deaths of the martyrs of the church
- Sexual practices of aboriginal peoples
- Geology, especially mineralogy, petrology, and pedalogy (the study of soil)
- Metallurgy
- Opera
- Lenses and microscopes
- Self-defence, several martial arts, and boxing
- Police procedures
- The British legal system
- The violin
- Classical composers
- The circulatory system

Things Sherlock Became an Expert in at University
- Illegal drugs
- Greek tragedies
- Roman tragedies

- Shakespearean tragedies
- Mythology
- Surveillance equipment
- Handwriting analysis
- Ink
- Statistics
- Chemistry
- The muscular system
- Serial killers and criminal profiling
- Cannibalism
- Firearms and shooting
- Tobacco and ash

Things Sherlock learned and immediately deemed unworthy of a place in the Memory Village
- Nursery rhymes
- Dinosaurs ("What do you mean, they're all dead?")
- Animals
- Astronomy
- History, in general
- Maths, other than statistics
- Nutrition
- Cursive Handwriting

Things Sherlock refused to learn anything about at all
- Sport
- Economics
- Popular culture: film, television, and music
- Philosophy
- Politics
- Poetry
- Etiquette
- Babies

Sherlock Now

"Sherlock, this is not an option. You are going. You're the guest of honour, for God's sake!"

There had been a series of threats made against six hospitals, a few suspicious packages left in emergency departments, and three fires set. The headlines screamed for weeks. Gi came to Sherlock after a particularly embarrassing article berating the Yard for its incompetence. After a trail of tips phoned in from anonymous sources, an examination of hospital payrolls, and a mad dash around the city, Sherlock had solved the case. It turned out to be a disgruntled maintenance worker who'd been transferred from hospital to hospital for his inability to get along with his colleagues. Finally, he was terminated and he sought revenge. Representatives from hospitals around the city were holding a luncheon to express "our gratitude for your commitment to the citizens of London."

"They made you a plaque!"

"John. A plaque. I don't need and I don't want a plaque. Or a luncheon. Actually, I'd rather eat the plaque than accept anyone's gratitude. There will be speeches John. You know there will be speeches and I will get obviously bored, which will upset people and then you'll want to give me a verbal thrashing. And I'll deserve it! Don't make me go, John. Please? In what conceivable scenario will this not backfire?"

Sherlock was right and John knew it. A crowded room, flashing cameras, the drone of conversation, clinking silverware, smells – it would drive Sherlock mad. Everyone would be jostling for photo opportunities, invading his space, and shaking his hand, putting their arm around him. John switched tactics. "These are my colleagues, Sherlock. I've worked at these hospitals. They're expecting me – us – to be there. It would be insulting to Gi not to show up! Besides, I'm so very proud of you and you never let me show you off." John snuck up behind him and grabbed him around the middle. He nuzzled into the back of Sherlock's neck and murmured softly. "Please, love? Do it for me?"

"That's cheating. You know I'd jump off a—"

"Oi! Shut it." John swatted his arse.

Sherlock turned to face him. "I'd do anything for you, you know it." He kissed the top of John's head. "It would be worse for me to go and embarrass you."

Sherlock looked thoughtful for a moment. "Maybe Lestrade could plant a few suspects as a distraction and I could concentrate on them. I could deduce—"

"*No!* We're not turning your luncheon into a crime scene, so forget it."

Sherlock huffed in frustration. "Well then, you're just going to have to figure out how to make me behave."

John had accrued a lot of experience running interference between Sherlock and the world. It had taken a while to figure out what kinds of settings triggered his defences and he'd learned to read his body language. Sherlock had a particular way of rubbing his fingertips together when he was trying to stay calm. His eyes would start flicking towards the exits. Sometimes he was able to contain himself long enough to send John a text surreptitiously, asking for a reprieve, and John would rescue him. It was an emergency when he edged up to John's side, eased his hand over, and tugged on his cuff.

This luncheon was important. It would boost Gi's standing at the Yard and definitely bring in new cases. Time for them to negotiate.

"All right. A minimum of three hours. An hour before, an hour for lunch, and an hour after."

Sherlock went on offense. "Three hours? Our wedding wasn't three hours!"

John rolled his eyes. "It was five hours and you don't remember half of it because you got quite merrily drunk, threw up on me, and couldn't have sex for the hangover!"

Attempting to retain his dignity, Sherlock replied, "Exactly my point. I couldn't bear more than two and a half hours without anaesthetising myself." He gave himself away with a lovely blush.

"Well, if three hours was your absolute limit, we'll set the bar at two and a half. An hour before, an hour for lunch, and half an hour after." John held up his hand to cut off Sherlock's protest. "*If* you behave, we'll see about leaving early. I'll ask Mycroft to phone us or something."

"And what if some dowager latches onto me and won't let go?" he asked petulantly.

"I swear on the honour of the Fifth Northumberland–"

"Never mind, just make sure you're there to rescue me, or I'll be storming out in dramatic fashion." He folded his arms and turned away.

John lifted the hair off his neck and kissed him. Then he licked a trail from there right up behind his ear. Sherlock shuddered.

Indulgently, John said, "I promise not to leave your side. And when we get home, you can have a special treat. Yes?"

Sherlock turned his chin over his shoulder, looking down at him and speaking with eyebrows raised and voice lowered. "What kind of treat?"

"Oh, I don't know, I suppose…if you don't like their dessert, I could serve you something at home that you'd prefer. Massage? Or maybe you'd like me to wear my uniform. Name your price. Or maybe you'd like to think about it while the presenters are blathering…"

There were some moments of silence, as the juggernaut of Sherlock's intellect stirred. John watched in admiration, pleased to have distracted him. Once the gears were engaged, Sherlock permitted his body to be steered over to the window, where John placed his violin in his hands. He plucked and sawed at the strings, while (John was certain) he considered prospective rewards.

The day of the tribute, John stood behind him, looking into the mirror and wrestling him into a tie. "Stop fidgeting! You're a grown man, you can wear a tie for three hours!"

Sherlock turned round and shouted back, "You said two and a half!"

Disgusted, John walked to the door, shouting as he opened it, "Mrs Hudson!" only to find her climbing the last stair.

All fancied up, she bustled in, patting John's hand and whispering, "Let me have at him."

In her most chiding, motherly voice, she said, "Sherlock, dear, really. What's the matter? Here, let me do that for you." She turned him around and knotted up his tie, chattering away and not letting him say a word. John stood scowling at him with his arms crossed, while she fussed over him, straightening his lapels and brushing invisible dust off his shoulder. She took his arm and whisked him right out of the flat, John following behind.

Between Lestrade, Mrs Hudson, and John, Sherlock kept within acceptable social boundaries. John ushered him from well-wisher to glad-hander when Sherlock's patience thinned. When John's frustration peaked, he handed him off to Mrs Hudson and got himself a drink. He picked him back up for some more mingling before passing him to Gi for the meal itself. With a final pinch to his arse, John warned him not to make faces at the food; he could cut it up into pieces and push it around on his plate if he couldn't bring himself to eat it. Then he reminded him to think about his reward. Sherlock got a dreamy look on his face and spent most of the meal in the Memory Village. The tablecloth hid his bouncing legs and he mimed attention to the speakers. Gi kicked him when he fidgeted too much.

John had given him a speech and ordered him to read it. Sherlock resented the insinuation that he couldn't memorise something so trivial. "You say exactly what's on that paper, nothing more, or less. If you want your reward."

He delivered the speech flawlessly and gave John a haughty look. John nodded approval. Plaque accepted, applause acknowledged, and post-presentation mingling concluded, the three handlers shepherded Sherlock out smoothly.

Once again, John had acted as Sherlock's social buffer.

John praised Sherlock effusively as they left. Gi went back to work after thumping him on the shoulder repeatedly and Mrs H. petted and fussed over him all the way home. Sherlock scotted, but they knew he was secretly preening.

Once the door was locked behind them, John pushed him up against it in a full body press and squeezed his arse. "I am so proud of you. I know it was hard, but you were brilliant. Whatever you choose, you deserve it."

Sherlock groaned and shifted his hips up against him. John pulled his head down and gave him a sloppy, wet kiss. More sounds issued forth and John pulled back to ask him, "What have you decided?" Sherlock disapproved of the space between them and grabbed John's head to resume the kiss.

"Well?"

"Whatever I want."

"Yes, I promised."

"No, I mean one hour. Whatever I want. No questions asked, no preconditions."

John looked at him sceptically. "You've nearly poisoned me several times, Sherlock."

Sherlock sighed theatrically, elongating his words, as if John were a young child. "Obviously, nothing that you would consider dangerous."

John stared suspiciously.

"Nothing public. Nothing permanent."

Sherlock waved his hand dismissively. "Brilliant, not insane, remember? Please, John, I was good. They gave me a plaque!"

Caving in, John pointed at him. "And no blood!"

Sherlock was so giddy, John began to regret his agreement.

"You look like you're about to be sentenced. Cheer up, John! We're going to have sex!"

John considered.

"Good point. Shall I shower?"

Sherlock narrowed his eyes and lowered his voice half an octave. "Be very thorough."

John swallowed and froze, a field mouse to Sherlock's fox, but it was too late. Sherlock stalked him, backing him up until he bumped into the wardrobe. Sherlock held a dressing gown, which he thrust up against him. "Fourteen minutes. I'm setting the timer."

John shoved a hand into his pocket, trying to rearrange his trousers, which appeared to be shrinking.

He took the entire fourteen minutes for his shower, trying to prepare for every potentiality, even as he knew it was futile. Who could adequately prepare for Sherlock? It had taken some time before he'd understood that sex could be fun, that playful was a good thing to be in bed. Once he'd let go of his ideas about 'the serious rules for sex,' his observation skills turned him into a responsive and creative lover. John delighted in almost everything he initiated, and it made Sherlock fearless. Which was a cause for concern at the moment. It occurred to John that a discussion about safewords might be a good idea.

The timer beeped.

With a delicious chill, John stepped from the loo to find Sherlock had stripped the duvet off the bed. He was holding a handful of John's silk ties. "Well done, Major. Fourteen minutes exactly."

John caught his upper lip in his teeth and fixed his eyes on the ties. They had played with restraints, but John had always been the one doing the tying. It wasn't that he was opposed. It just hadn't happened. Yet. John was so much more experienced and confident in bed, that Sherlock usually let him take the lead. John saw that Sherlock was momentarily shaken at his hesitation and John acted immediately. He stepped forward and said, "Tell me what you want."

Sherlock's relief and delight warmed John's heart. "Thank you, John." John grabbed his face and pulled him down for a smouldering kiss.

"I have a feeling I'm getting just as much of a reward as you are. Only you deserve it more. You were so good for me." Sherlock blushed at the praise despite himself and adopted a no-nonsense attitude as cover.

"All right. Naked. On the bed. I promise to go slow and you can say stop at any time. I promise you'll enjoy yourself. I know I will."

Sherlock taking control. Cold or excited and maybe both, John shivered the tiniest bit.

John dropped his dressing gown and sat on the bed, feeling particularly naked. Or maybe vulnerable? He reminded himself that he trusted Sherlock with his life. It was ridiculous to be anxious about his plans for the evening. His own words echoed in his head: *Don't mistake excitement for anxiety.* He smiled and lay down with his hands clasped behind his head. "All yours. Now and forever."

Sherlock glowed. He sat down on the other side, picked up the timer and set it for an hour. That glow was so enchanting and evanescent, John didn't want it to dim. He took the timer and removed the battery. "I don't think an hour will be enough." Sherlock's face lit the room and John's love for him warmed them both up.

Naked, Sherlock crawled over him and braced his hands either side of John's head. With no time limit now, he allowed himself to dither over which part of his face to kiss, then just began on the upper left and covered every inch of it. When he reached the chin, he stared down at that beloved face and wondered what was filling the back of his throat and prickling his eyelids. In the schoolroom of the Memory Village, he wrote a note (investigate choking sensation triggered by beloved face) on the blackboard.

Sherlock knelt over John and took his left hand from behind his head. He laid it on his thigh and looked questioningly at him. In response, John felt around on the bed with his other hand, and when he found the ties, he smiled and gave them to Sherlock, who smiled back. Gently, reverently, he picked up his wrist and kissed his pulse point, then proceeded to tie his arm loosely to the headboard. "Are you comfortable? Your shoulder?" John moved his arm to test his range of motion and nodded.

Pleased, Sherlock continued, kissing each of John's ankles before securing them to the footboard. He stood back to observe his handiwork and John waved at him and said, "Haven't you forgotten something?"

"Honestly, John. Me? Forgotten something? No. I want you to be able to touch me. Not anything else. Only me."

John took a deep breath through his nose and clenched the fist that wasn't tied up. That one free hand made him feel so much more restrained. Sherlock licked his lips and said, "But I get to touch all of you." And he proceeded to do just that. He straddled him again and placing his hands on the crown of John's head, like a blind man, he felt his way over the landscape of his strong, sturdy body.

As Sherlock moved his hands from one place to another, he could sense John's tension ratcheting up. Sherlock was as thorough in the touching of John's skin as he was in examining a crime scene. He was painstakingly slow. The difference in texture between the hair on his chest, the hair on his head, and the hair of his eyebrows had to be catalogued. The skin on the side of his neck was so different from the skin over his ribs. He touched no overtly sexual organs, but it didn't matter. Everywhere he touched made John twitch or tremble or sigh. If the timer had still been running, he would only have made it to his navel.

John kept a tight grip on Sherlock's hair, shoulder, whatever he could reach, but by the time Sherlock had finished with his leg, John was pulling his bound limbs towards him as well. When John couldn't reach him with that one hand, he began to whimper, the absence as profound as if they were in different time zones. Sherlock reached a hand back up to him and said, "Hush. I'm here." Sherlock began kissing and nibbling and licking where his fingers had been, and John's whimpers turned into moans. His cock was positively bouncing, leaving a puddle of pearly fluid on his taut belly.

John couldn't stop his hips from following Sherlock's wandering mouth. The lack of contact was making him ache. Sherlock smiled smugly and in between nibbles and licks of John's hips, he reminded him, "Don't pull like that, you'll rub yourself raw."

John grunted, "Sounds good." Not quite sure what he was asking for, John twisted against the silk, begging, "Sherlock, god, I'm losing my mind, please, please…hurry…"

"My reward. I get to take my time, remember?" He sucked hard on the inside of one knee, scraped his teeth over the crease of his thigh.

"I know, I promised," breathless, John said, "But you're so good, I can't wait, you're too clever…your…mouth, I can't, I–"

Sherlock gazed up at him, the wrecked look on John's face filling him with pride. Love swelled in his throat and he rasped, "Soon now, I won't be able to wait either."

John clenched the sheets with his free hand, writhing, trying not to touch where he wasn't allowed, but Sherlock saw his struggle and twined their fingers together.

Sherlock rubbed his throbbing cock against John's as he stretched up and bent his head to rub his lips teasingly over John's throat, eliciting groans. When he lifted his head, he saw red and purple spots he'd left behind, and lapped wetly everywhere he'd sucked and bitten.

It wasn't just sensation shivering through John. It was the intensity of focus, that concentrated mental energy all directed toward him, that was electrifying. Sherlock was touching, smelling, and tasting every surface of him he could reach, committing every sensation, John's every response, to memory. If John needed proof of Sherlock's love, there it was. Not many things could hold the interest of Sherlock Holmes; he, John Watson, was one of them.

Sherlock had begun breathing rapidly. "I've collected as much data as I can just now. We'll save the rest for another reward."

John was vibrating with anticipation. "Please, I'm so ready…" He trailed off groaning when Sherlock lapped up the puddle on his belly. He let go of John's hand and descended to lavish his attention on eight particular inches. All the power of the great engine was directed through his mouth. He dragged his tongue up John's cock from base to crown in one long slow lick. When he reached the head, he rubbed it with his cheek and covered every bit of it with his lips just to feel the softness. He exhaled, sniffed deeply and flicked his tongue out like a lizard, at the slit. John's frontal lobe tapped out. He could no longer form sentences, but it didn't matter. Sherlock wasn't listening to the babbling.

He was engulfing the head of John's cock with his mouth. He let his tongue slide around it slowly, adding a new sensation of texture to the Memory Village. Silk? Satin? He dragged his tongue down underneath then pulled off to lick across John's perineum and around his bollocks.

He took them into his mouth and investigated thoroughly before returning to swallowing as much of the shaft as he could. John had been on the edge so long, Sherlock knew there wasn't much time left. He licked his finger and circled around John's arsehole. John whimpered. Sherlock sucked in his cheeks on the upstroke and swallowed as he dropped down. There was no controlling himself now and John thrust up with each of Sherlock's movements, grunting, "Yes, yes," until Sherlock felt the pulsing that was his cue to pull off and stroke John with fist and tongue until he spilled onto his stomach. Sherlock came six strokes later.

When he caught his breath, he looked down at John and said, "You are so beautiful right now."

John gasped out a laugh and said, "Right. I stink of sweat, I've got bruises all over, and I'm covered in come."

Sherlock collapsed on top of him. "Beauty is in the eye of the beholder, me, and I say, you are beautiful to behold."

17

Sherlock Then

> Search terms: Asperger's or autism+ social
> skills+ delayed, deficits; social-emotional
> reciprocity; reduced sharing of interests,
> emotions; failure to initiate or respond
> to social interactions; difficulty+ sharing
> imaginative play, making friends; solitary
> play

Mummy loved Sherlock, but she couldn't wait for the day he could go away to school. When the doctor recommended that they wait another year, due to Sherlock's delayed social skills, her heart sank, despite her best intentions. He had to point out to her that Sherlock still sucked his thumb. This was not the sort of thing that would help him make friends, or even allow him to go unnoticed.

When the time finally came, it was even worse than the doctor had warned. Sherlock was taunted mercilessly, well beyond the typical boarding school teasing. He learned early on how to seek revenge that went undetected, but he was not able to figure out how to avoid the behaviour that prompted the teasing in the first place. He was awkward in groups and couldn't or wouldn't follow the simple rules of fitting in. He didn't know how to play the games they did and didn't care to try to learn them. It was difficult for the adults to tell whether he preferred to entertain himself or he had no other options.

He was self-contained and never sought anyone out except for the upper school's chemistry teacher. He cared about topics that other nine-year-old boys found mind-numbing and he refused to listen to things he considered boring. He couldn't be bothered.

The older he got, the more quickly Sherlock read and processed information. He was so efficient, he could learn a semester's material within a month and developed a strategy that enabled him to sit through classes without being distracted from his own agenda by irritating teachers. He would pay just enough attention to be able to answer one or two questions thoroughly. The teacher, convinced he was engaged, would ignore him for the rest of the period. Undisturbed, he would bury his nose in his own work. He covered ten times as much material as his classmates and outstripped every student, and eventually every teacher in every school they made him attend.

Thanks to his extraordinary memory, he excelled at test-taking but struggled with essay writing. He found it difficult to restrain his contempt and sarcasm and couldn't fathom the idea that he had to explain the obvious to teachers who should have known more than he did about said topic. It was pure torture. Mycroft begged him to take at least major exams and papers seriously. "It might impact your getting into university. That's where you're finally going to find the people who may be able to keep up with you. Where you'll be able to do the research you want to do."

For Mycroft, he made the effort begrudgingly.

Sherlock was mystified by his peers as a child. As adolescents, they were alien life forms. Any vestiges of logical, predictable behaviour disappeared in the face of their hormonal impulses. They professed love for one another, then pinched and smacked and ran away. Tiny snubs toppled alpha teenagers and turned them into sobbing wrecks. Simple friendship was difficult; puberty was a minefield. He deepened his isolation to forestall more painful rejections and felt stable by comparison.

Adults kept saying that he would find his tribe, believing his peers would catch up with him at the next school level, but Sherlock lost the drive for social interaction long before his childhood ended. He wasn't particularly interested in a tribe. The cost benefit analysis left him unmotivated. The more effort he had to expend to establish contact, the less he enjoyed the company. He did make attempts to integrate himself into groups, but it was unclear whether he wasn't trying hard enough or just didn't need the companionship. When someone intrigued him, he had to decide if it was worth disguising his real self for a few moments of engagement. Once he dropped his guard, he assumed the charade would be over and he'd be found wanting.

In the end it didn't matter. There weren't that many people he didn't find mind-numbingly boring.

```
Search terms: Asperger's or autism+ difficul-
ties adjusting behaviour to social contexts;
absence of interest in peers; conversation-
al ability; peer rejection; social+ limited
participation, communication, withdrawal
```

The students who'd known Sherlock in primary school ignored him for the most part, believing he preferred it that way. By secondary school, Sherlock believed it himself. He was meant to be alone. He had no need for other people. There was no counter evidence and he stopped questioning his isolation. Eventually he just stopped trying.

Mummy and Daddy saw no indications of distress. He'd always been solitary. His lack of a social life didn't seem out of the ordinary compared to Mycroft's. Sherlock interpreted his occasional loneliness as boredom and when it struck, he picked up his violin or wrote some music or examined something under his microscope. It was just another sensation that he learned to ignore, like hunger, fatigue, or illness, vague discomforts that he tried to ease intellectually. It was a misattribution of stimulation and he looked for relief in the wrong places. His neurological cross-wiring made it impossible for him to describe his perceived experiences and he had nothing to compare them to. A child who is colourblind does not know what 'red' is. They know it means something to everyone else, but it has no meaning for them. A child born without a limb believes their body to be perfect as it is. They feel no sense of longing for what they've never had before.

```
Search terms: Asperger's or autism+ deep
pressure; weighted+ blanket, vest; low tac-
tile sensory threshold; altered tactile
processing; social touch aversion; touch+
hypervigilance, avoidance
```

He was untouched. Theirs was never a hugging family. He had no friends to tussle and scrap with. There were unavoidable social interactions that he suffered through by necessity, but he resisted any gratuitous touch: handshakes, hugs, kisses on the cheek. Physical contact with others disappeared from his life completely. It was a gradual enough process that it did not register as a loss.

Part of it was ordinary maturing. Once he could walk away from Mummy, he rarely returned. He had always been prickly but now he stiffened at her touch. In response, she tried to touch him ever more lightly, but he perceived her stroking and tickling as an irritant.

As a child he refused to wear constrictive clothing, but now he wore a heavy coat earlier in the fall and longer into the spring. He thought about getting a cat for the sensation of a warm body next to his and slept under the weightiest blankets he could find, year-round, trying to satisfy the primal human need for touch. He took up boxing, relishing the deep impact of fists pounding into the heavy bag and thudding into his flesh. It soothed the unidentifiable itch temporarily. He sought out gravity and pressure to stabilise him, ground him to the earth, and keep him from floating off like a balloon.

As Sherlock's body matured, he discovered another yawning gap between himself and the boys at school. He suffered the same hormonal upheaval and physical discomfort and was subjected to his body's urges as they were, but knew almost immediately that he was different yet again. They spoke constantly and solely about girls. Sherlock hardly noticed their absence.

His sexual orientation was not just a social liability. It left him swirling in confusion, contorting himself to conform at this most fundamental level, fighting against his body as he always had. He texted Mycroft after his first wet dream and was comforted to know that, as usual, his body was functioning 'normally.'

Just like his vision, hearing, intellect, the mechanisms were intact – it was just his perceptions that were atypical. He did not address the content of the dream, already aware that he deviated from the norm. Was he among two? four? ten? percent of the population? Was he the only one at his school?

Sherlock was hyper-aware of his own attractions. Curves and softness held no appeal, no matter how he tried to focus his laser-like attention. He was all about edges and planes: broad chests, narrow hips, and bony knees. Muscled thighs and sculpted abdomens.

He desperately hoped no one would notice his preference for wide shoulders, deep voices, and beards.

His dissembling skill sharpened as he struggled to hide his attraction to male classmates. Mycroft needed no details. He already knew. He implemented a plan of normalisation for Sherlock immediately. Works by Oscar Wilde and about Alan Turing appeared on his nightstand. Massive coffee table books of Warhol and Mapplethorpe were left strategically around the house. Sherlock was not fooled.

"You've figured it out then."

Mycroft, canny as ever, unsuccessfully feigned ignorance.

Sherlock sneered. "I'm gay. You knew before I did."

Mycroft abandoned the effort. "No reason you should conform

in this any more than you have in any other arena, little brother. Just another adaptation you must make. Of course, you always have the option to opt out."

"What are you talking about, opt out?"

"You don't have to play the game. You can abstain from the struggle to create relationships. It's served me well so far. You have a hand. You don't need a partner. Your body serves at the pleasure of your mind. Or I could find you a vetted playmate."

Sherlock was torn between a gut-level instinct to flee from the agonisingly awkward conversation and the habit of heeding Mycroft's predominantly useful advice. He didn't know how to be with anyone so maybe, he thought, he should learn how to be alone.

Mycroft gave him the basics.

```
Search terms: Asperger's or autism+ sexu-
ality; relationships+ deficits+ developing,
maintaining, understanding; social+ compe-
tency, isolation; sexual+ intimacy, arous-
ability
```

"Aside from...colleagues, one could say...I am alone. And I prefer it. I certainly don't have friends."

Sherlock nodded and then carefully approached the real question. "So, you've never..." That was as close as he could get.

Mycroft spared him. "Yes. I have on several occasions engaged in sexual activity with another person. Physical desire can be quite compulsive. It was enjoyable. Pleasurable, no question, but ultimately the effort to establish the prerequisite emotional connection outweighed the physical satisfaction. Intimacy requires a certain degree of unfeigned interest, and sadly, as you know, interesting humans are quite rare."

"Intimacy." Sherlock repeated in a long and drawn-out manner. "I thought that was the point."

"Not physical intimacy, Sherlock, emotional intimacy."

Sherlock repeated, "Emotional intimacy. What does that mean? How is it achieved?"

"Oh, exchanging meaningless reports of the day's events, questions about one's feelings, the sharing of private information. Trivial detail of one kind and another." He sighed. "The monotony... Never understood the point, but that is what's expected in long-term sexual or so-called romantic relationships. And you, Sherlock, will have more difficulty than I do, navigating through the subtleties."

Sherlock agreed with the assessment. Mycroft didn't enjoy the games, but he knew how to play.

Sherlock didn't understand the rules. He couldn't even stay on the field. He was forever out of bounds.

18

Sherlock Now

John's laptop was missing once again. It was one of those occasions when John couldn't decide if Sherlock was acting on purpose or whether it was just another of his perceived entitlements. Muttering to himself, he rummaged on the desk, the coffee table, the kitchen table, and under the slippery stack of papers and journals, where he found Sherlock's tear off calendar pad. He had been looking around for it yesterday. The bygone days were folded over. Yesterday's page was still on top. It had some scribbled addresses written on it, but on the bottom right-hand corner, in uncharacteristically neat handwriting, were the words, "Hold hands." Puzzling. He folded the page back to expose today and there in the same corner, was "Offer snack." Flipping to tomorrow, there was another, "Hand on shoulder."

Thursday, "Head in lap," Friday, "Suggest walk," Saturday, "Ask about movie night." He unfolded the bygone days and the notes continued: fingers in hair, tidy fridge, squeeze knee under table, note in briefcase and then, with a certain suspicion, he turned to February 13th. All caps: BUY FLOWERS. He breathed in sharply. John remembered. Sherlock had bought flowers. The next page said, "Red."

They were reminders. Sherlock had written himself a year's worth of reminders, a guide.

A manual on loving John, a how-to book for a beginner.

John was sorely tempted to peek into his future, but he was brought up suddenly and shamefully. The weight of Sherlock's intention pressed on his conscience. He considered the effort it must have taken him, the great shift in his understanding, to manifest his mysterious and unsettling emotions in concrete physicality. To translate love into an actionable plan. Sherlock didn't think about the future. He'd never made a New Year's resolution in his life, but here, the thing he had decided was worth the effort, was John. Conflicted at first, he wasn't sure if he should let Sherlock know he'd stumbled across his to-do list. He'd clearly meant it to remain a secret.

A childhood memory rose, the Christmas Eve of his tenth year, when he'd accidentally found the presents that his mother had hidden so carefully. He'd had the brief impulse to crow a victory. He'd been right! There was no Santa Claus! But with a flash of insight, a glimpse into his coming maturity, he recognised the effort she had taken to preserve the mystery for him and his brother. He closed the closet door and let Christmas unfold, its innocence intact. The intent of the giver suddenly meant more to him than the gifts, and the act itself, more precious.

He buried the calendar back where it belonged.

Sherlock Then

One afternoon, during Christmas holiday, Sherlock came home from a day in the woods with his eyes dulled and went immediately to bed. No one noticed until dinnertime when Daddy sent Mycroft to fetch him. He found his little brother in the dark, under the bedclothes, moaning and rocking, with his hands clutching the sides of his head. Mycroft was so alarmed, he didn't even try to figure it out by himself. He ran downstairs, crying, "Something's wrong with Sherlock!" and not being a young man prone to overreaction, both his parents responded immediately.

Mummy turned on the light, and, truly frightened, Daddy tried to uncover him. "Sherlock, boyo, what is it? Talk to Daddy. Let me see. Please."

As soon as he exposed him, Sherlock cried out, "It hurts! The light hurts!"

Mummy turned it off and Daddy tried again to find out what was hurting him. Sternly now, he said, "Tell me where it hurts."

He moaned, "My head, my head, there's something in my head."

Mummy called the paediatrician, while Daddy tried to see what it might be. He pulled him upright and Sherlock vomited into his lap. The doctor said he'd meet them at hospital and Sherlock was bundled into the car and driven there with his head in Mummy's lap, body stretched out on the backseat.

They arrived at A&E before the doctor but Sherlock, moaning and rocking, was not prioritised. A child with a headache but no fever didn't raise an eyebrow in triage. He covered his eyes immediately against the harsh lights of the waiting room. Mummy wrapped her scarf around his head to help. Daddy rocked him and stroked his hair. When the doctor arrived, he ordered some scans and blood tests but barring any head trauma or concussion, he concluded that it was a migraine and that there was very little he could do for him.

The frequency and intensity of the headaches increased throughout puberty and although there were some identifiable triggers, they were mostly unpredictable. Sometimes he saw flashes of light, floating circles, or lines across his field of vision. The blood cascaded loudly through his veins. It was different from his synaesthesia, but he was used to coping with atypical sensory experiences and was grateful for any warning of an oncoming headache.

When the pain struck, Sherlock drew the blinds, and tried to sleep as much as he could. No medication worked, not painkillers, not vasoconstrictors. Sometimes he asked for heat packs, other times, ice packs, and other times, he just moaned until it ended.

The doctor remarked, "We'll have to consider it another mysterious feature of his remarkable brain."

Sherlock was no stranger to pain. Since infancy, his comforts had been complicated. Sleeping was a struggle. Food triggered reflux.

Physical contact was soothing at the perfect intensity, otherwise unbearable.

And then he grew up. No one chased after him to see if he was okay, whatever okay was. When puberty attacked, it was only stubbornness that kept him sane. Otherwise, his baseline was centred somewhere around excruciating, a persistent scraping of sandpaper against the grain of his nervous system. If he were sufficiently intellectually engaged, the constant prickling receded to tolerable.

Eventually heroin helped him focus his ravenous awareness, but when the coke wore off and there was nothing to grind between the wheels of the great machine, the engine had to be stopped. If pure strength of will couldn't halt it, heroin was the only respite. He sought distraction, numbness, and as last resort, oblivion, the drift off the edge of blinding lucidity. The melting into black emptiness was a relief. He was able not to think.

It was so precious, to be able not to reason, to watch the logic drift and fade. To float in sensory impressions that were uncomplicated by suffering, the eventual crash too dim and distant to worry about.

There was no price too steep to pay for the peace and absence it brought.

Peace. He feels peaceful and…happy? It's warm. And soft. And safe.

From very, very far away, he hears someone calling. Mykie? Mycroft. Calling him. He sounds so…bossy. Everything with Mycroft is so important; so urgent. He was resting and calm and now Mycroft is making him nervous. Part of him wants to go back. Mykie is always right and he would be angry if Sherlock didn't come. Mummy said, "Mykie will always take care of you." Daddy said, "Always listen to Mykie." And he almost wants to. He does. Because Mykie shelters him. He trusts Mykie. He makes it better sometimes. But it's so warm. He wants to cry because he doesn't know what to do. He can't decide. The way back is covered with

KAMEO LLYN DOUGLAS

glass, sharp needles of glass, the light crackling off them, shrieking as it scrapes against itself, driving shards and spikes into his skull.

There must be some reason Mycroft is making him come back, but he can't think of what it might be. If it were important, Mykie would come get him, wouldn't he? There's no pain where he is. No chattering, no hissing boredom, no itch under his skin.

But Mycroft is making him come back. He hates him for making him come into the light, up from the dark, back, out of the bliss.

He knew it. Flashing red blue screeching crackling stabbing at his brain, through his eyes and ears. Something shaking him, a slap across his face. Sherlock tries to burrow back down into the waves of stillness, but there's pressure on his chest and the air is rushing in and he doesn't want to go.

Someone is screaming his name and he doesn't want to listen, but it's Mykie and he has to listen or Mykie will be angry with him and he bursts through to awake, sobbing, "No, no, no," and his eyes open and Mycroft is crying on him, getting him wet and he closes his eyes again, but, fucking Mycroft, he doesn't stop...

Sherlock woke up in hospital, connected to tubes, and hurting. His head still worked so he turned it and saw Gi rubbing his eyes. Mycroft was stretched out beside him, sleeping. When Gi noticed that Sherlock was awake, he startled and shook Mycroft's shoulder without taking his eyes off the hollow-eyed skeleton in the bed. He walked slowly to the side of the bed, holding back rage. "Say something."

"I'm too tired."

"Do you know how close you came this time? They said there might be brain damage. You almost didn't come back at all."

"I didn't want to. He should have just let me be."

Mycroft and Gibran Lestrade met the first time at St Bart's while the nurse was trying to find a vein of Sherlock's sturdy enough to draw blood through. One of the Inspector's officers had found the boy, sixteen, needle still in his arm, nodding in an alley in

Hammersmith. He had an "In Case of Emergency" card in his pocket and Mycroft beat the ambulance to A&E. He identified the man in charge in his usual efficient and unremarkable way and led Lestrade to an empty office in seconds. Whatever was said, when Sherlock was stable, Mycroft had him in his first rehab with no police record on file. Although Lestrade knew when he'd been beaten and wiped the official slate clean, his personal sense of responsibility wouldn't let him rest. As soon as Sherlock was permitted visitors, he made his way there and took the boy, kicking and screaming, under his wing.

Mycroft was startled to cross paths with him again after the third overdose and, concerned by the Inspector's over-involvement, he casually invited him for a cup of tea. The inspector, being a clever sort, understood immediately that there was nothing about Mycroft that could ever be considered casual.

Knowing when he was outmatched, he laid his cards on the table. He could never have won with the bluff.

"Here's what you know. Your brother's eighteen. He's brilliant. He's in no danger from me, but without something to occupy his brain he'll kill himself very soon. Here's what you don't. I might be able to keep him alive."

Mycroft had had the background checks done and knew Lestrade was above reproach and more intelligent than most of his peers, but he was still sceptical. How could a policeman possibly save his brother from himself? His face, as ever, gave nothing away.

"I freely confess to my inadequacy. Please. Enlighten me."

"Have your minions discovered why he hangs around my borough?"

Mycroft's underlings had in fact tracked his movements, but Sherlock's knowledge of the surveillance made him cagey about camouflaging his activities. Mycroft struggled to keep his irritation concealed but Lestrade's semi-smirk told him they hadn't been as wily as he'd hoped.

"Since you're in homicide, it must have something to do with murder, but unless I'm misinformed, he's yet to commit one. What have I missed, Mr Lestrade?"

"Inspector Lestrade. He solves them. He sees things no one else can see. He's a strange, brusque, uncommunicative burr beneath my saddle, but he solves murders nobody else can. And it makes him happy. When was the last time you saw your brother happy?"

The eyes staring back at him were bleak.

Mycroft looked off into memory. "He was twelve. His paper was accepted for *Chemical Science*, the flagship journal of the Royal Society of Chemistry. He was the youngest contributor ever."

Gi shook his head. "I won't even pretend to understand. I wanna take him on as a consultant. When we can't figure something out. The position doesn't exist. Don't know if it's possible to create it. I can't do it myself, don't know anybody – official – who could make it happen, but I suspect…" He trailed off. He handed Mycroft a small stack of folders. "He's already made me look better than I am. I figure it could be mutually beneficial. Plus, I'd have an excuse to keep an eye on him and he'd have to put up with it."

Mycroft tilted his head to the side and drew a business card from his inner pocket, shook Inspector Lestrade's hand and left.

The next day an envelope appeared on the Inspector's desk, containing a sheet of paper with a single word on it: Done.

He showed it to Sherlock.

"I won't be an office boy. You'll ask me for help and I'll decide if I'll investigate a case or not. Only interesting ones."

Even from his hospital bed, unable to stand, wearing a diaper, with tubes up his nose he was bossy.

Sherlock Then

It took a year for Sherlock to mention that he had parents, let alone think of introducing them to John. He was actually shocked when Sherlock mentioned offhand that he was thinking about visiting them for the weekend.

"Your parents? They're still alive?"

"No, I'm visiting their corpses. Of course, they're alive. Whatever would make you think they were dead?"

John puzzled it over for a moment. "Well, I don't know. I suppose I've just never heard you talk about them. You speak to them?"

Sherlock widened his eyes. "We speak every week! I speak to them more often than Mycroft does. Why wouldn't I speak to them? Do you think I blame them for how I turned out? Do you think they've disowned me?"

"Don't be ridiculous. If your parents didn't murder you in your sleep as a child, I don't imagine there's much you could have done to make them disown you. I expect they're proud of you in fact." John looked him up and down and considered. "And no. I don't think you blame them. What would you blame them for? You're happy with who you are for the most part, I think. And you should be. I am. You've never mentioned them, that's all, not once, and I assumed they had passed on. It's just a little…bizarre."

Sherlock wondered whether he should be offended but decided that it was bizarre. He thought he ought to be grateful to have a boyfriend who didn't mind bizarre. He agreed, it was rather unusual, and he was fortunate to have parents who tolerated his peculiarities and rarely complained.

Sherlock hadn't appeared to notice the holidays when their first Christmas came round; after they had settled into the unspoken understanding that they were together, whatever that was going to look like. John asked what they would be doing.

"What do you mean doing?"

"Doing for the holiday, as in going anywhere, seeing anyone, having guests."

Sherlock waited.

"Christmas! How will we celebrate Christmas, Sherlock? We are going to celebrate together, aren't we?"

Sherlock's eyes widened. "Of course we are! I mean, I assumed we were going to. That is, if you want to."

John smiled and shook his head at him. "Yes, of course. I want to. What else would I do?"

"You do have a brother."

"I'd rather have an excuse. And you are an excellent excuse. So, what are we going to do? What do you usually do?"

"I go to see my parents. They've invited us."

"Well, then. If you're not ashamed of me—"

"They're expecting us on Thursday."

John raised an eyebrow.

"I accepted on your behalf."

Sherlock was looking forward to the holiday, an experience he'd forgotten. He knew his parents would love John – adore him, even more in person than they already did from Sherlock's descriptions. They were overjoyed to have someone – anyone in his life. Mycroft wasn't worried for him anymore, so they weren't either.

He was stable. They weren't listening for that call in the night that could only mean disaster. Mycroft assured them the worst was over and they had John to thank.

They were thrilled to host him, to get a first-hand look at the man taking care of their boy, and eager to meet someone who saw in Sherlock what they had always seen.

"It takes genius to recognise genius! Bring him home! I want to shake his hand."

Sherlock rolled his eyes. "I am rolling my eyes at you right now, Daddy. There's no need for hyperbole. Honestly."

Mummy continued. "I'm so glad he's coming, Sherlock. I can't wait to meet him."

"You're both being ridiculous. He's just a man. Granted, a doctor. And soldier. Quite steady and reliable in an emergency. Unbelievably tolerant and forgiving…"

Daddy prompted, "Yes? Go on."

"Oh, never mind. We'll be there Thursday."

"The sooner the better!"

"Hurry, darling."

He hung up.

"Do you always hang up on your parents?"

Sherlock stared at John blankly.

He was confused for a moment. "Oh, that. The goodbye. Don't worry. They don't take it personally. They don't expect it. We made an agreement when I was about…thirteen, I think. I told them I had learned the mandatory protocols of social interactions, but they were pointless. And draining. I proposed that home be neutral ground. They should assume that I was being polite and respectful to them whether I was or not. I promised I would be polite in the real world, when it mattered. They agreed immediately and I was quite reliably polite. When necessary. For the most part. Until I moved out."

John narrowed his eyes at him. "You're rude to your parents."

"No! Not rude. Not offensive or insulting or mean. Just…not polite."

John sat down. "I'm sorry, but I'm not as clever as you. You're going to have to explain this to me. Isn't being rude the opposite of being polite?"

"John. My parents are remarkable people. Clever of course, but infinitely patient. They raised me without once resorting to violence. Mycroft was an unusual child. He might have been a challenge to average parents, but he and my mother were temperamentally very well-suited to each other. However, I am not suited to anyone. I was unbearable. Impossible. A horror."

"Oi. No talking down the boyfriend."

It was a rule. Sherlock ignored it as usual.

"And of course, during the bad periods, I put them through hell. I was a nightmare. Worse than I was as a baby which was horrible. They never gave up on me."

"I can't imagine you as a teenager. Shudder to think."

Sherlock nodded. "It wasn't pretty."

His anxiety ramped up prior to the visit, but John tried to keep it all low-key.

"Relax, Sherlock. It's going to be fine."

He was pacing and mumbling to himself, never good signs. "What if…Suppose–"

"Stop it! Look at me." John grabbed him by the shoulders and lowered his voice. "Nothing terrible is going to happen. Your parents will like me. I will like them. For chrissake, your brother likes me, and he barely likes anybody! And I already like them for growing you into yourself and keeping you alive so I could find you someday. The next time I see you fretting, you're in for it. If you can't clear your head, I'll clear it for you. That's your only warning."

It took two thrashings, once after a shopping trip where Sherlock couldn't decide on the proper colour of a sweater to give as a gift to his mother, and once after Mycroft wound him up about them sleeping in his old bedroom.

They left Sherlock as clear and fresh as the air after a thunderstorm. They also relaxed John. They gave him a feeling of control and relieved his own anxiety. He did believe he would charm Sherlock's parents and he had a great affection for them already. He knew they were brilliant. But he also admired the strength and determination it must have taken to support their boy through his struggles with his demons. It might be stressful, but he was confident he could keep Sherlock stable. It was only for a few days, and they'd certainly been in worse situations.

The visit exceeded everyone's hopes. John and Daddy spent hours wandering in the woods and Mummy found in John someone who not only loved her little boy, but ate anything she cooked. She opened her long-neglected box of recipes and John joined her in the cooking. Sherlock could hear them whispering and giggling, quickly cutting off when he came near. He pretended to be irritated, but he felt something else: the sensation of comfort, being around people who knew him, all of him, and loved him not in spite of it, but because of it. His parents, his brother and his partner, and now John. He belonged with these people. They were his. His family. And John's presence strengthened the bond.

He didn't have to monitor his behaviour. It was impossible for him to offend them and he was freed from the tangled chains of social niceties. Against everyone's expectations, he actually behaved better. As in more conventionally. His lack of anxiety enabled him to pay more attention to the meaningless subtleties of good manners. He wasn't focused on his own potential missteps. And he knew they wouldn't judge him when he did, inevitably, get it wrong. They'd laugh or put him right and they wouldn't hold a grudge. And he enjoyed watching them together. He always enjoyed watching John, of course, but watching him interact for the first time, with people he knew so well, gave him new insights. He saw John forge new relationships in live time. He observed how they responded to him, how he used their feedback to make connections in areas they had in common. He noticed and identified the intricacies of encouragement and acceptance between them. He isolated specific skills ("May I help you with the dishes?" "Tell me more about your time in Vienna." "Was that really you at the Yard that afternoon?") that John used to learn who they were, and he could see how they liked him for it. He was a witness to the beginning of their relationships – present at their birth.

On the final day, Daddy invited Sherlock for one last walk through the woods. For a while they shared a comfortable, familiar silence. Daddy tried to pretend that he wasn't smiling at him every few steps until Sherlock stopped, irritated.

"You're too old to play Cheshire Cat. What is it?"

"We always knew, your mother and I. Never had any doubt. And you outdid our expectations, as usual."

"Stop being cryptic! What are you talking about?"

Daddy poked him in the chest.

"Now who's playing? Doctor Watson, of course. We always

knew you'd find someone. And you did it." He poked him again. "You took the risk and let him in. You allowed it to happen, Sherlock, and I'm so proud of you. Yes, brilliant." He waved his hand. "But that came naturally, it was never an effort for you. It's easy to shine in your areas of strength. This, however. This required great courage on your part, I know, and you did not falter. You met the challenge."

Sherlock stalked off to hide the flush of pleasure he felt at hearing his father's praise. "You're being ridiculous again."

Daddy just laughed at him.

"We want him back. Soon and often. Bring your Scotsman home for New Year's Eve, Sherlock. I've always wanted to hear Auld Lang Syne in authentic brogue."

19

Sherlock Now

It was one of John's casual expressions of frustration with a typical act of Sherlock's habitual disregard.

He'd left toxic chemicals in John's favourite mug. As John scrubbed it more viciously than absolutely necessary, he muttered, "Had they already stopped canings by the time you went to that public school of yours, mister?" Out loud and pointedly he said, "Can't help but wonder if a couple of decent spankings would have nipped all this in the bud."

It was a throwaway line, no more irritated than his usual admonishments, and John couldn't understand why Sherlock wasn't ignoring him as he usually did. Not only was he not ignoring him, he was frozen, staring at him with his lips slightly parted.

"Sherlock, what's the matter, why are you staring? Do I have something on my face?"

"Say that again."

"Say what again?"

"What you just said."

"What, about spankings?"

Puzzled, John rinsed, then dried his hands. He took a few steps closer to him. "That's an interesting reaction you're having there, Sherlock. I'm going to say the word again, just to see what happens." He moved in on him, predatory and prowling. Sherlock couldn't help but back up, his eyes open wide and fixated on the beloved, dangerous man stalking him.

From chest to cheek, a blush sprang up, in full bloom.

Pinned against the wall, head between his surgeon's hands, Sherlock felt like John was looming over him, despite his lack of height. He gripped Sherlock's hair and gently but firmly tugged his head down. He said it again, under his breath and right into Sherlock's ear, "Spanking. Is that what it is, Sherlock? Do you need a spanking?"

As he watched, Sherlock's jaw dropped and his eyes rolled back in his head, eyelashes fluttering closed. John smirked and pressed his advantage. He drew his finger down Sherlock's neck. "Well, look at that. All this time, I've been nagging and shouting, taking care of your messes myself, and all I had to do was threaten you with a spanking? I think we should try it. What do you think, Sherlock?"

Sherlock was finding it difficult to speak. Or to think. The blood seemed to have left his head entirely.

"I'm wondering if I haven't been firm enough in my requests. If perhaps I should have been insisting on your compliance and perhaps making my displeasure known at your disobedience. And since the word itself seems to have made an impression on you, I think we should see what an actual spanking might accomplish. And I think we should do it right now."

With a shuddering breath, Sherlock choked out, "You know best."

John took him by the hand and dragged him to the sofa. He sat and held him between his knees. "Now, let's review. Have I asked you before not to use my mug for your experiments?"

Sherlock stared at him and John repeated himself and prompted. "Yes or no, Sherlock."

"Uh, yes?"

"You don't sound certain. Have I asked you not to use—"

"Yes. Yes, John, you have," Sherlock blurted out.

"There's a good boy."

Sherlock gasped and now *John* froze. "Oh, my. You liked that, didn't you? You liked me calling you a good boy. Did you like that, Sherlock?"

Sherlock swallowed and closed his mouth. He looked away from John's intense stare and nodded quickly. John resisted the urge to press him for actual words and vowed to explore the issue further. He had more pressing matters to attend to.

"Take off your shirt and vest." With shaking fingers, Sherlock complied. John reached for Sherlock's belt and began to unbuckle it. Sherlock stared down open-mouthed. He undid the button, then zipper, then lowered his trousers. John took his hand and drew him down over his lap, but then twisted slightly so Sherlock could rest his chest on the sofa. "Lanky git. We'll have to figure out a better plan. Maybe over a chair. Or get you a bench."

Sherlock shuddered and John grinned. He rubbed small circles so that the pants rubbed over Sherlock's skin, tickling him and raising up the fine hairs on his back.

To set a sterner mood, he growled, "Now. Tell me why you're getting a spanking, Sherlock."

"Wha – what?"

"Don't play games, I asked you a question. If we're going to do this, we're going to do it my way and we're going to be very clear about what we're doing. So. Tell me why you're getting a spanking."

"Th-the mug?"

"What about the mug?"

"Toxic. Chemicals. In the mug. I'm sorry, I'm sorry, John."

He pulled Sherlock's pants down over his round, white arse. He stroked the pearly skin and gooseflesh spread from his thighs to the back of his neck.

"That's right. You put chemicals in my mug. And now I'm going to spank you for it. And then I'm going to forgive you for it. And the next time you're tempted to use my mug for anything other than tea, you're going to remember this spanking and how disappointed in you I was. And you're going to use one of the tins that I stored under the sink just for your experiments."

It was a very long speech to listen to while turned up over someone's lap with a naked bum.

But now that John mentioned it, Sherlock realised he was sorry he'd disappointed him; John, who did the shopping because Sherlock had used up all the milk; John, who made sure there were clean mugs for tea, no matter what Sherlock had put into them; John, who had asked him twenty times at least, not to use his mug. Couldn't he remember to use the tins that he'd collected for him?

At first, he didn't recognise it: regret? Remorse. It was remorse. "You're right, John, and I am sorry. And I'm going to remember next time."

"I believe you, love. I believe you will. And we're going to see if I can help you. If you'll let me try. Will you let me try?"

Sherlock swallowed and said, "Yes, John. Please."

John lifted his hand and let it fall. The noise registered first. It startled both of them. John stared at the pink flush spreading over china-white skin while Sherlock was still struggling to locate himself in time and space. John gathered himself and adopted a conversational tone, expressing faith in Sherlock's good intentions, his ability to change his behaviour, consider John's feelings, etc.

By the time the sting of the first blow reached Sherlock's consciousness, John was spanking with gusto and a wave of heat and contrition was already building.

John kept the rhythm of the rise and fall of his hand steady, and although he'd suffered much worse from violent men seeking his destruction, this pain cut more deeply, straight through to Sherlock's heart.

He was ashamed, not just of the childish position he was in, but that he had provoked John so – the man who loved him without reason. This pain, and it was painful, no childish spanking, differed from the helplessness of injury from an enemy. This was pain with purpose, pain he'd chosen to accept, like a refinery's fire, burning away impurity and imperfections, leaving a finer grade of metal behind.

He thought of the man whose lap he was laid over and the pain led him to remorse. He touched his face and didn't recognise his own tears for a moment. He began to huff out heavy breaths and missed the sound of John's voice. He needed to hear it and he offered, again, "I'm sorry, John." Silence. The hand continued and Sherlock tried rephrasing. "I am very sorry—" he gasped as John changed the focus of his blows "—that I used the mug—" John increased the speed but remained silent and Sherlock gave up his restraint and let the tears flow.

John continued until Sherlock was unable to speak for the bawling.

It was catharsis more than anything else. The self-consciousness was what brought down the wall. Sherlock's psychological propensity was to detach himself from physical pain. He prided himself on his ability to disregard his body. The mortification of a spanking split a hairline crack in his façade and then the physical pain triggered his emotions to bubble up and out.

The confusion of being literally upended had him looking at things from a different point of view. It forced him to confront his actions and John's responses to them. In his current position, they couldn't be ignored or dismissed as sentiment. Arrogance offered no defence. So, John let him weep until he felt some of the tension dissipate. He pulled him upright and Sherlock clutched him like a drowning man.

"It's going to be all right, love."

"No! It's not. I'm an awful person. How can you love me?" Great wracking sobs.

John hardened his voice a bit and said, "I just do. Even when you're an arsehole."

Sherlock looked up at him, eyes red and streaming, nose dripping, a complete mess.

John pushed the sweaty hair away from his forehead and kissed him tenderly. Sherlock struggled to catch his breath and John heard a meek voice come from his throat for the first time.

"How can you?" he asked, bewildered.

Sherlock Then

Mummy was afraid to take Sherlock most places. She found him unpredictable and it was difficult to concentrate on errands when she took him along, so she didn't. She didn't have the knack of distracting him the way Daddy did. He could anticipate a coming storm and for the most part steered him in another direction before the thunder and lightning began. Mycroft seemed to have a sixth sense about it.

Sherlock wound up staying home by himself and they both preferred it that way. During periods when Daddy was away on business and Mycroft was at school, Mummy and Sherlock saw one another only at meals. The rule had always been that Sherlock could read at the table. It was a compromise to keep him there; he hardly ate. The meals were quiet, occasionally silent, but never unpleasant. As Sherlock matured, he became conscious of Mummy's reluctance to be away from home with him. Once on one of Mycroft's phone calls, Mummy heard him chattering away about the events of the week.

"Oh, no. Mummy doesn't like to take me places anymore. I don't think she likes me around much at all. When are you coming home again? That's a long time, Mykie."

Mummy took to her bed with headache and Sherlock and Daddy had a companionable dinner. And breakfast.

Once Mummy recovered, she resolved to help Sherlock understand what it really meant to love someone. She knew that bringing up the topic too close to the event would backfire. He knew he was different from other children. He hated creating scenes and always apologised afterward. She couldn't fool him, so she waited. The time came when, on another of his frequent phone calls, Mycroft complained bitterly about his literature course.

"There is nothing redemptive in it. Not a scrap of science! Utter nonsense. 'We are such stuff as dreams are made of.' It's incomprehensible!"

"Perhaps we should read along with Mycroft, little man. Literature is not his strength. He finds it extremely tedious, but you might maintain his interest. I'm sure your insights will be valuable. And you know Mykie. If he thinks he's teaching you, he'll be delighted."

They shared a secret smile.

"He likes to be the expert, right Mummy?"

"You're such a good brother, to let him think so, Sherlock." She risked putting her arm around his shoulders. To her great relief and satisfaction, he leaned into her and taking advantage of his lowered defences, she bent down to take in his little boy smell: the scent of his hair, the earthy smell of dirt ground into the knees of his trousers.

To her rescue: The Bard.

The Comedy of Errors, Act 1 Scene 1

EGEON

My youngest boy, and yet my eldest care,
At eighteen years became inquisitive
After his brother, and importuned me
That his attendant–so his case was like,
Reft of his brother, but retained his name–
Might bear him company in the quest of him,
Whom whilst I laboured of a love to see,
I hazarded the loss of whom I loved.

It was The Comedy of Errors that gave her the opportunity to introduce the subject. After one of Mycroft's literature calls, Sherlock came to her to share the highlights. Struggling under its weight, he brought the eleven pound "Collected Works of Shakespeare," and opened it to Act One, Scene One. Grinning brightly, he chirped, "Look, Mummy! Mykie said Shakespeare was writing about me!"

He pointed to the line, "…my youngest boy, and yet my eldest care…"

"That means even though I'm the littlest one, I'm the biggest problem." Mummy felt her heart tighten up. She closed the massive volume and took him by the hand into the garden. She headed for the hanging swing. It was best to broach serious conversation with him while sitting side by side, rather than head on. His capacity for companionship or concentration was greatly reduced when he was expected to look directly at someone.

"We all know Mykie is quite intelligent, but this time he was only half-right, Sherlock. You are my youngest boy, but you are most certainly not a problem."

"He was just teasing me, Mummy. But I am a problem. What about the argument with Mrs Fletcher? And the muriatic acid on the countertop? And the museum? Mykie never makes fusses like that. I'm little but I can be a big bother."

"You are little. Are you old enough to keep a secret? I would tell you if I knew you'd never tell."

"I can keep a secret. You can trust me."

"Hmm. Well, you mustn't ever tell him, but Mycroft was a very boring child."

Sherlock smiled from behind his hand. "He's still boring sometimes, Mummy." They giggled together.

When they had finished sharing the joke, Mummy said, very seriously, "You are never boring, Sherlock. And I like you that way, even if it means there are a few fusses occasionally."

"I think I understand, Mummy. I hate to be bored. I'd rather think about a problem than have nothing to think about."

"Agreed, but I want to be very clear about something Sherlock, so please, I'd like to look at you directly."

He swivelled so Mummy could see into his eyes.

"I love you. I will always love you. There is nothing that you could do, not even the most terrible thing imaginable, that would change my love for you. No one on earth could make me stop loving you even if they tried. Even if I tried to stop loving you, I couldn't. You'll hate hearing it, but no matter how old you get, you will always be my baby. Just the way Grandmama thinks of me as her baby."

"A mother's love isn't influenced by her child's behaviour or age or anything else, Sherlock. You are precious, a gift from the universe, a unique, one-in-seven-billion miracle. Of course I get irritated sometimes. You are extraordinary. No mother alive could understand you well enough to never be irritated with you. Sometimes I worry that I might not be taking proper care of you. I hate it when I don't know what you need, or how I can help you when you're suffering. It makes me feel so helpless because all I want to do is keep you safe and happy. You can't imagine the love I feel for you." She placed one hand on his cheek and with the other, moved aside the hair from his forehead and kissed him there. She savoured the moment, knowing there would be a limited number of them coming in the future.

When she sat back in the swing and began to rock slowly, he did the same, then inched closer to her so that their arms were not quite touching. They did nothing for a while, just enjoyed the peace and each other's presence.

"Can I tell you the story of something that happened a long time ago? I promise it's true."

Wide-eyed, Sherlock nodded.

"All right. You might find it difficult to believe.

"Once, when you were very small, still in your pram, we were walking and, I'll never forget. It was February but a warm day with the bluest sky. Like your eyes, I thought. A day promising spring."

She smiled when she saw that his mouth had dropped open just the slightest bit and the dreamy look had come over him.

"We waited at the crossing and there was a bus waiting at the traffic signal along our side. And a car that was waiting to turn onto Windham Road. And because I knew the bus was going to move alongside of us and that the car had to wait to turn, I started to cross. But the driver of the car had forgotten or didn't know that Windham is a two-way street and he turned in front of the bus. And I saw him coming and I knew, I just knew, Sherlock, that he was going to hit us. And do you know what happened?"

He shook his head, and she continued.

"Without a conscious thought, immediately, my arms jerked and pushed the pram out of the way."

Sherlock's eyes widened and he was completely alert. Mummy looked at him intensely.

"The car stopped." She held out her arm. "One cubit away. I could have reached out and touched the bumper."

Sherlock mimicked her movement and they remained like statues for a moment, then lowered their arms in tandem. "Do you know where you were?"

He shook his head again.

"On the other side of the crossing."

The curious look came over his face. "You pushed me all that way?"

"Yes."

"Without thinking?"

"Yes."

"Weren't you afraid of the car, Mummy?"

"Oh, yes, Sherlock. Terribly afraid."

"Why didn't you run?"

"As you said, I didn't have time to think. But my arms knew what they needed to do to keep you safe."

Silence.

"Because you love me?"

"Yes. More than I can even think about. The deepest part of me, the part that's deeper than thinking, loves you. I love you, Sherlock." She waited.

"I think that must be true. There are no other conclusions to be drawn from the facts. I'll think about it some more, but really, what else could explain it?"

"I'm very glad that you agree with me. I've thought about it for years now and I can't think of any other theories to explain the evidence. Those are the facts and so it must be true."

She checked on him that night and was surprised to find him sleeping. She hoped that it was because she had helped him lay down at least one of his burdens.

Sherlock Now

"Who knows how anybody loves anybody? But I do. And you're going to learn how to be more thoughtful of the people who love you. Because being thoughtless hurts you too, even if you've ignored it before. You feel bad about it now, don't you?"

For a stoic man, he was crying very easily. "Yes, I feel bad. I wish I hadn't done it. I…feel regret." He sounded a bit surprised.

Realisation came over his face. "I don't want to make you unhappy." He clutched again and John pulled him close, whispering in his ear.

"There you are. Crying? Feeling regret and this resolving to act differently? That's catharsis. When you calm down, you're going to feel so much better. Lighter and easier."

Sherlock looked back at him again with a quietly disbelieving look. John felt himself tearing up and chuckling at the same time.

"Yes, believe it or not, you're going to want to apologise instead of feeling like it's some meaningless chore you have to do."

Sherlock nodded quickly.

"And I'm going to forgive you, and it will be over. You'll start again and try to do your best and I'll help you. Because I love you." Much quiet crying was followed by a trip to bed, where Sherlock slept for an unprecedented seven hours, his mind blissfully blank.

John learned the signs. Sherlock would provoke him subtly with minor annoyances that set him on edge: using his toothbrush, misplacing his razor. A day or two of screeching on the violin, leaving contaminated lab equipment in the tub. When John found himself gritting his teeth and fighting the urge to shout, he'd realise that he was on edge because Sherlock was on edge. He needed John to reset him, but didn't know how to ask. He needed John to take over.

And whatever Sherlock needed…

Resurrecting the soldier he'd thought he'd left behind in the desert, he lowered his voice and let it rumble across the flat.

"Enough, Sherlock. Time to relax." Sherlock Holmes had never relaxed in his life. It was a ridiculous notion, except it was code, an offer that Sherlock could ignore if John's instincts had missed the mark.

When he saw the gratitude in Sherlock's eyes and the loosening of his shoulders, John knew he was right. "Bedroom. Strip and kneel."

Sherlock's neurons had always been crossed. His pleasures had always been mixed with pain. The ecstasy of heroin began with the tightening of the rubber tourniquet and slapping of the vein, the bite of the needle. The heroin stung before it thrilled.

As gentle as John longed to be, Sherlock craved the throb and burn.

That was how John tamed the craving, on nights when Sherlock could find no other way to extinguish the flames crawling up his spine. He came to John with hollow eyes pleading for release from the restraints that kept him operating as precisely as the gears of a watch. When the springs were coiled properly, he kept time like the sun rose, but when the crown had been over-tightened, the pieces were likely to grind against one another and leap out of the case.

Only John could set him right, could tease and surprise him with sensations he couldn't predict. John showed him he didn't have to analyse them, that their randomness could free him from the tyranny of his never-ceasing intellectual instrument.

The drip of hot wax, the strike of a flogger, a spanking that brought him to tears; pain loosened the tension inside him.

He chased after the ache and sting, latched onto it with his singular focus and it quieted the constant noise jangling along his nerves. He trusted John enough to allow him to overwhelm his body with a mixture of pain, pleasure, and endorphins that lifted him, floating, in a cloud as soft and warm as heroin's. Unlike the poison, John left him in a place that drugs never could: in stasis, at peace, and balanced.

Part of the relief was the release of responsibility; the chance to stop thinking. Part of it was the absolution. The pain was an aspect. The humbling. There were so few times Sherlock felt he could rely on someone else's dominance, in any sense, not in his usual dismissive way, just as an objective point of fact.

It was a relief to humble himself before John. He could relax and luxuriate in this tremendous boon, something that only John could do for him. He could submit and relinquish control because he trusted John to take him down and then bring him back up without diminishing him or costing him any of his sense of self. It was surrender without loss, a victorious submission.

And Sherlock rose from it with renewed energy and a clear mind. Denied the responsibility of choosing or making decisions, he was set free. It was a recalibration.

It brought John peace as well. Sherlock, indisputably, was difficult to live with and presented daily, sometimes hourly, challenges for a typical person to endure. He had always struggled with the concept of boundaries, overstepping them constantly. Their sessions allowed catharsis for both of them. It eliminated John's need to express his irritation in spirit-crushing, relationship-destroying nagging and grudge-holding and it helped clear Sherlock's conscience. It returned them to baseline.

They kept a running tally of John's irritations and Sherlock's transgressions. It was difficult for Sherlock, but John required him to articulate them at the time of the correction. It was important that he make the connection between his actions and John's feelings. They didn't need formal rules. Sherlock knew what John expected. It was an honour system and the punishment, usually a spanking, but sometimes harsher, always ended with a rapprochement of affection and forgiveness and frequently, memorable makeup sex.

It was like spring rain, or a summer downpour that cleared the haze and smog from the city and brought a cool clarity back to their home. A generosity of spirit.

John's sense of duty made it almost impossible for him to knowingly annoy Sherlock. He created as much of a haven for him as he could. Sherlock couldn't reciprocate but John didn't mind. The things that Sherlock brought to their partnership were unique and John valued them far above the triviality of domestic tranquillity.

The whole of humanity chafed Sherlock like a wet bathing suit that he couldn't wait to get rid of. John was honoured to know that he was the one person he turned towards. He was honoured to be the sun to his sunflower, and that Sherlock would lay himself across his lap, soul and bottom bared.

20

Sherlock Then

Daddy waved off the doctor's mention of autism, and dismissed the concept outright.

"What's the point in labelling him? We've tried speech therapists and counsellors and he was smarter than all of them. How could they help him? What's the purpose of pursuing a diagnosis if there's nothing to be cured?" Daddy resented the implication that there was something wrong with Sherlock. "And what are we trying to fix exactly? There might just as likely be something wrong with everyone else, that we find him irritating! Maybe our puny intellects are too limited to cope with his extraordinariness! Maybe we're just inadequate!"

The doctor recommended perhaps, a social skills group, but Mummy couldn't imagine trying to wrangle him to any more appointments. They just made him crankier. Mycroft did some research and concluded, yes, probably Asperger's Syndrome. But, so what? He concurred with Daddy. He had always loved and defended his baby brother. Now he respected him in the way he respected anyone who spoke a language he didn't: as the possessor of great and hidden secrets that he might never learn. If he was exceptional, why should they try to change him?

When he began to research the syndrome himself, Sherlock acknowledged that many of the diagnostic criteria matched what he considered to be his finest qualities.

Disability? Impairment? Bollocks.

American Psychiatric Association's Diagnostic and Statistical Manual of Mental Disorders, Fourth Edition

Asperger's Disorder (299.80)

Diagnostic Criteria

A. Qualitative impairment in social interaction, as manifested by at least two of the following:
  (1) marked impairments in the use of multiple nonverbal behaviours such as eye-to-eye gaze, facial expression, body postures, and gestures to regulate social interaction.
  (2) failure to develop peer relationships appropriate to developmental level.
  (3) a lack of spontaneous seeking to share enjoyment, interests, or achievements with other people (e.g. by a lack of showing, bringing, or pointing out objects of interest to other people).
  (4) lack of social or emotional reciprocity.

B. Restricted repetitive and stereotyped patterns of behaviour, interests, and activities, as manifested by at least one of the following:
  (1) encompassing preoccupation with one or more stereotyped and restricted patterns of interest that is abnormal either in intensity or focus.
  (2) apparently inflexible adherence to specific, nonfunctional routines or rituals.
  (3) stereotyped and repetitive motor mannerisms (e.g., hand or finger flapping or twisting, or complex whole-body movements).
  (4) persistent preoccupation with parts of objects.

C. The disturbance causes clinically significant impairment

in social, occupational, or other important areas of functioning

D. There is no clinically significant general delay in language (e.g., single words used by age 2 years, communicative phrases used by age 3 years).

E. There is no clinically significant delay in cognitive development or in the development of age-appropriate self-help skills, adaptive behaviour (other than social interaction), and curiosity about the environment in childhood.

F. Criteria are not met for another specific Pervasive Developmental Disorder or Schizophrenia.

American Psychiatric Association's Diagnostic and Statistical Manual of Mental Disorders, Fifth Edition

Autism Spectrum Disorder (299.00) [F84.0]

Diagnostic Criteria

A. Persistent deficits in social communication and social interaction across multiple contexts, as manifested by the following, currently or by history (examples are illustrative, not exhaustive, see text):

(1) Deficits in social-emotional reciprocity, ranging, for example, from abnormal social approach and failure of normal back-and-forth conversation; to reduced sharing of interests, emotions, or affect; to failure to initiate or respond to social interactions.

(2) Deficits in nonverbal communicative behaviours used for social interaction, ranging, for example, from poorly integrated verbal and nonverbal communication; to abnormalities in eye contact and body language or deficits in understanding and use

of gestures; to a total lack of facial expressions and nonverbal communication.

(3) Deficits in developing, maintaining, and understanding relationships, ranging, for example, from difficulties adjusting behaviour to suit various social contexts; to difficulties in sharing imaginative play or in making friends; to absence of interest in peers.

Specify current severity:
Severity is based on social communication impairments and restricted repetitive patterns of behaviour (see Table 2).

B. Restricted, repetitive patterns of behaviour, interests, or activities, as manifested by at least two of the following, currently or by history (examples are illustrative, not exhaustive; see text):

(1) Stereotyped or repetitive motor movements, use of objects, or speech (e.g., simple motor stereotypies, lining up toys or flipping objects, echolalia, idiosyncratic phrases).

(2) Insistence on sameness, inflexible adherence to routines, or ritualized patterns or verbal nonverbal behaviour (e.g., extreme distress at small changes, difficulties with transitions, rigid thinking patterns, greeting rituals, need to take same route or eat food every day).

(3) Highly restricted, fixated interests that are abnormal in intensity or focus (e.g., strong attachment to or preoccupation with unusual objects, excessively circumscribed or perseverative interest).

(4) Hyper- or hyporeactivity to sensory input or unusual

interests in sensory aspects of the environment (e.g., apparent indifference to pain/temperature, adverse response to specific sounds or textures, excessive smelling or touching of objects, visual fascination with lights or movement).

Specify current severity:
Severity is based on social communication impairments and restricted, repetitive patterns of behaviour (see Table 2).

C. Symptoms must be present in the early developmental period (but may not become fully manifest until social demands exceed limited capacities, or may be masked by learned strategies in later life).
D. Symptoms cause clinically significant impairment in social, occupational, or other important areas of current functioning.
E. These disturbances are not better explained by intellectual disability (intellectual developmental disorder) or global developmental delay. Intellectual disability and autism spectrum disorder frequently co-occur; to make comorbid diagnoses of autism spectrum disorder and intellectual disability, social communication should be below that expected for general developmental level.

The benchmarks fit. Sherlock had failed to develop peer relationships, not that he hadn't tried. He had shared his pleasures and interests. It's just that no one else was interested. He pointed out matters of interest constantly. He frequently took off on long flights of discourse, waxing eloquently and passionately on scholarly topics never mentioned outside of a graduate studies symposium.

He was met with blank stares and polite trivialities. After enough rejections, his failure to initiate or respond to social interactions was completely understandable. The further isolated he was by the disinterest of others, the less he cared about adjusting his behaviour to suit various social contexts. He had no fear of social disapproval, but he learned to keep his fascinations to himself.

Deficits in understanding relationships: to put it mildly. He was clueless.

The absence of interest on the part of his peers led to the absence of interest in his peers. They ignored each other. Didn't that qualify as social or emotional reciprocity?

Hyper- or hyporeactivity to sensory input? Compared to whom? Was it a disability to notice what others ignored? Or ignore the irrelevant?

He exhibited stereotyped speech. Unfortunately, his vocabulary and phrases were too difficult for the inferior intellects surrounding him to understand.

He was intense – abnormally so? According to the banal general public?

Autism?

Bullseye.

Sherlock Now

They end still on the sofa with Sherlock curled up, his face buried in John's belly, strong arms wrapped around him. His voice is muffled, but the grief leaks through. "I don't deserve you, John. I'm broken. I've always been broken. You'd be better off–"

"Sherlock! Stop it." John's voice is stern, and Sherlock hears it in his chest. John stands and gently lays Sherlock's head down. "Stay put."

He returns carrying a bowl and the rug from the floor on his side of the bed. He reaches over for the blanket from the back of the sofa. He puts them all on the coffee table.

"Deduce for me, Detective. What do they have in common?"

Sherlock begins. "Islamic prayer rug, back from Afghanistan,

Navajo blanket, bowl is Japanese, in the Kintsugi style, the cracked pieces joined–" He cuts off and stares up at John. "They're all imperfect. Intentionally imperfect. The rug has a flaw woven in by the artist because only Allah is perfect. The pattern in the blanket is disrupted by a spirit line so the weaver doesn't become trapped in the work. The bowl has been repaired with lacquer and gold, to make it more beautiful than it was whole. They are all broken."

John smiles at him. "And all the more precious for being broken.

"Everyone is broken, Sherlock. There's just more broken like me. We lie, we can't remember anything, we're oblivious, disorganised – but you. You are rare and wonderfully made. You are broken unlike anyone who's ever lived. You're broken perfectly, and if they, if I forget that you don't think like ordinary people, that's my fault."

"But–"

"No, listen. You think I'm not broken?" He touches his shoulder. "Rumi, a Muslim, said 'The wound is the place where the light enters you.' A believer would say I was blessed, Alhamdulillah," John says, fingering his rug. "I wouldn't change anything, not being shot, not the misery afterwards…it brought me to you. Of all the lives I could have lived, this one, ours, is the one I'd choose. You. Are the one I would choose."

He stretches over the objects on the table and kisses Sherlock gently. Then bites him, hard. "I'm not saying you're not an infuriating, maddening pain in the arse and that I don't frequently want to murder you, but nothing worth having comes easily and you are worth having. I want all of you. You wouldn't be you without every single bit of you and of all of those bits, I love the broken ones the most."

He holds up the bowl with the golden cracks. "They're the most beautiful."

Sherlock watches his husband and feels the love behind his words, that irrational love without explanation, that he had seen but never thought possible for himself. He thinks about what his life would have been without that love, without the man who saw things in him that he didn't think were there and drew them out, into the light so that he, himself could see them. And he gets an idea.

The next day, before John wakes up, he goes out, and later when he texts, Sherlock won't tell him where he's gone. Three hours later, another text. This time the answer is, 'I went to get some dirt. BRB.'

Having heard many such nonsensical explanations, John says to himself, "Ah. Of course."

When he gets home, true to his word, Sherlock has a bag of dirt. A two-gallon zipper-locked bag of dirt.

"New case? Gi didn't call."

"No, silly, I wouldn't leave you behind on a case. This is a gift. For you."

"You bring me a bag of dirt as a random gift, and I'm the silly one."

"Well, I admit, it doesn't look like much, in truth, it isn't much, but it's not finished yet, so you'll have to be patient."

"Oh, I see. Not finished yet. Right."

Sherlock kisses him and says, "Just don't touch the bag."

John catches glimpses of him working with what he assumes was the dirt in the bag, but Sherlock is very secretive about it and covers it with a towel whenever he comes near. He keeps his back to him, and John can see his arms moving, but it is impossible to sneak up behind Sherlock Holmes, so he doesn't bother trying.

"Is it clay? Are you making a mug? A vase?"

"Wait and see. You don't really want to know, do you? If I tell you it will spoil the surprise. And you're supposed to be the patient one."

Sometimes he hums while he works, sometimes he watches the telly, but other times it takes up his entire attention. The bag spends the night in the refrigerator a few times and that almost brings an end to the project completely.

"Sherlock, what did we–"

"Don't move it! Don't even touch it. It's at a very delicate stage of the process, John, and if you disturb it, I'll just have to start all over again. Please."

The 'please' signals the significance of the project and John bites his tongue.

When Sherlock can see that his patience is gone, he calls John to the kitchen table.

"I wanted you to see that I've made progress." With a great flourish, he uncovers…a ball.

"What did you do? It's perfectly round!"

"Don't touch! It's not finished. Give me a little more time. And don't go doing any research."

John backs up. "Okay! Promise."

Two days later, he hands John a gift-wrapped box. "It's very fragile. Be gentle."

Carefully, John takes out what he assumes is the same ball. But now it is perfectly smooth, glossy, almost glowing.

"It's…like a marble! How did…you did that? Varnish?"

"Hikaru dorodango. Shining mud ball. Traditional children's pastime. Not difficult. Dirt and water and loving care. Shaping, drying, polishing, that's all. You see, I was thinking about the Kintsugi bowl." He picks it up. "It just wasn't right. I'm not the bowl. Before you came, my life was more like a bag of dirt."

John interrupted. "Don't–"

"No. Wait. It was a life but without shape. There was no beauty there. Not a life that anyone would choose. It wasn't until you came. You took me as I was and loved me into a new life. So, I think you're the Kintsugi. You may have been broken, but now…" He picks up the bowl, gently rolls the dorodango into it, and kisses his husband.

For the rest of their lives together the objects hold a place of honour, the shining sphere of mud nestled in the broken golden bowl.

The End

Acknowledgments

My son. You know who you are. You always have. I wish I could take some credit for your creation, but overall, I think I had very little to do with it. You were your own perfect self from the moment you existed, and you never let anyone stand in the way of your choosing who you would become. I am proud to have been able to participate and watch it happen.

Kyndall and Tom, you know the whole of me and are still here. Thank you for your never-faltering support and encouragement. You made me braver than I ever thought I could be.

Wendy, thank you for making me believe it was possible and then making it happen.

I could not have written this book without the lessons I learned from the children on the autism spectrum who guided me throughout my career. Thank you all for letting me in.

About the Author

Kameo Llyn Douglas (Kristine Polisciano) began writing professionally at the age of 55, thanks to Sherlock Holmes and John Watson. As a special educator and literacy coach, she spent much of her thirty-seven-year career teaching teachers to teach writing to students with disabilities. Their unique characteristics inspired the version of Sherlock Holmes in her first book, *Rare and Wonderfully Made* with Improbable Press.

You can find Kameo on Twitter and Tumblr as KameoDouglas.

She lives with her remarkable son and their three-legged dog, in Brooklyn, New York.

Resources

The Autistic Brain: Helping Different Kinds of Minds Succeed
Temple Grandin and Richard Panek

Uniquely Human: A Different Way of Seeing Autism
Barry M. Prizant

The Complete Guide to Asperger's Syndrome
Tony Attwood

NeuroTribes: The Legacy of Autism and the Future of Neurodiversity
Steve Silberman

Look Me in the Eye: My Life with Asperger's
John Elder Robison

There's a Boy in Here: Emerging from the Bonds of Autism
Judy Barron, Sean Barron

How Can I Talk If My Lips Don't Move: Inside My Autistic Mind
Tito Rajarshi Mukhopadhyay

The Reason I Jump: The Inner Voice of a Thirteen-Year-Old Boy with Autism
Naoki Higashida

Get More Great Stories

ImprobablePress.com

From ancient gods rising, to road trips on the trail of cryptids,
from romance to mystery to adventure,
Improbable Press specialises in sharing the voices and tall tales of
women, LGBTQIA+, BIPOC, disabled, and neurodiverse people.

Come along for the ride.

Sign up for our newsletter *Spark* at
improbablepress.com

Find us on Twitter @so_improbable
Instagram @improbablepress

www.ingramcontent.com/pod-product-compliance
Lightning Source LLC
Chambersburg PA
CBHW032204190626
46810CB00018B/1550